D0944242

Floating Illusions

Other books by Chelsea Quinn Yarbro

Locadio's Apprentice
Four Horses for Tishtry

CHELSEA QUINN YARBRO

Floating Illusions

1 8  1 7

HARPER & ROW, PUBLISHERS

Cambridge, Philadelphia, San Francisco, London, Mexico City, São Paolo, Singapore, Sydney

NEW YORK

The *Duchess of Malfi* and her passengers are all fictitious, although based on ships and persons of the time. However, none of them are, or should be construed as representing, actual persons, places, or events. Those locations that are real are used as fiction, and events of the period are referred to for verisimilitude only.

Library of Congress Cataloging-in-Publication Data
Yarbro, Chelsea Quinn, 1942–
Floating illusions.

Summary: Shortly after fourteen-year-old Millicent meets an intriguing stage magician on board an ocean liner, the cruise is disrupted by a series of apparently impossible murders.

[1. Magicians—Fiction. 2. Ocean liners—Fiction. 3. Mystery and detective stories] I. Title.
PZ7.Y1954Fl 1986 [Fic] 85-45825
ISBN 0-06-026642-2
ISBN 0-06-026643-0 (lib. bdg.)

For
the distinguished Italian basso
Cesare Siepi
with admiration and affection

ACKNOWLEDGMENTS

In the four years I worked at the unique nightclub the Magic Cellar, in San Francisco, I was privileged to see many fine stage and close-up magicians, and to them all I owe much of the theatrical magic used in this book.

In particular, I would like to thank:

PAUL and MARY LOU SVENGARI, who provided me with specific information about stage magic in 1910, and

CEDRIC and JAN CLUTE, who owned the Magic Cellar and gave me access to the many illusions of Carter the Great.

1

"Oh, look!" hooted Aunt Mehitabel as the green automobile with the brass fittings threaded its way through the dockside traffic. "It's Haywood's Briarcliff! His tourer!" She clasped her hands together and leaned against the rail, waving energetically.

"He can't see us, Aunt Mehitabel," said Millicent in her low, sensible voice. "If he tried to look, he'd probably hit one of the carriages."

"But he'll have to find us," protested Aunt Mehitabel as she continued to wave.

"He knows what deck we're on, and we don't sail for another two hours," Millicent reminded her, sighing a little in spite of her admonition to herself not to be upset at this latest return to Europe. She had been crossing the Atlantic twice every year since she was nine and often told herself that she ought to be used to it by now.

The Lozier Briarcliff was eased into a narrow parking

space in front of the largest warehouse, and as his sister and daughter watched, Haywood Brougham Cathcart descended magnificently from his vehicle. He looked at the towering sides of the *Duchess of Malfi* and directed his gaze toward the first-class deck.

"He sees us!" exclaimed Mehitabel, her waving increasing. "He's looking for us."

Dutifully Millicent leaned over the rail, her straw hat slightly askew, and waved. "He'll be with us shortly, Aunt," she said quietly.

"Isn't it exciting?" Mehitabel demanded of the air, and was answered by a tall, well-dressed gentleman standing a few feet away.

"Setting off on a sea voyage is always exciting; I agree." He smiled at Mehitabel and then added diffidently, "Forgive me for speaking, but I always feel that sharing the same deck constitutes an introduction. It is as if the *Duchess of Malfi* herself has introduced us."

Mehitabel was flustered and flattered. "I suppose . . ." she began, then cast a look down into the busy confusion on the dock, as if wishing for her brother to decide for her. With a rare gesture of social daring, she looked back at the gentleman, moving her parasol so that she could show off her dashing hat and extend her gloved hand. "I daresay you're right. I am Missus Reyns and this is my niece, Millicent Cathcart. We are going to Switzerland after landing at Genoa."

The man smiled. "How charming. I am Mister Wingham, Geoffrey Wingham, at your service."

"No doubt we shall see much of each other," Mehitabel went on, feeling quite reckless.

"On a ship, it is likely," he agreed, a twinkle in his dark eyes. "Is this your first sea voyage?"

"Oh, yes," enthused Mehitabel, then she added, "but my niece is quite an old hand at it by now. She has been traveling between New York and the Continent for five years."

"My," marveled Mister Geoffrey Wingham, "what a well-traveled young lady."

"My mother lives in Europe," Millicent said. "I go to school in Switzerland."

"Indeed," said Mister Wingham; then he bowed slightly to Mehitabel and turned away, saying as he did, "I look forward to visiting with you."

Mehitabel watched him stroll away from them down the deck, and fussed with the light shawl she wore to keep the sun off her lovely pale skin. "He is . . . somewhat forward, of course," she remarked to her niece, "but quite charming. It must be the setting."

"Possibly," said Millicent, and in the next instant her attention was claimed by the arrival of her father.

Haywood Cathcart was a large, robust man, dressed in sporting tweeds and cap, his thinning brown hair shiny as shellac with brilliantine, and his slightly old-fashioned moustache waxed and curled to perfection. "Sorry about the delay, my pet," he said to his daughter as he took his sister's hands. "There's nothing but carriages the length of Park Avenue, and none of the other streets are any better. It's the weather. Everyone wants to be out before the storm comes. It's getting very close."

"Gracious, yes," said Mehitabel, not quite simpering. "I have been feeling the heat for days."

"You'll be cooler on the ocean, I hope," Haywood Cathcart said to both his sister and daughter. "There's so much going on below. Stewards and stevedores rushing here and there. It's that damn . . . dashed magician fellow."

"What dashed magician fellow?" Mehitabel asked, both irritated that she knew nothing about it, and excited to hear of it now.

"Oh, some theatrical person with his troupe. They performed at the Lyceum last week, I believe." Haywood Cathcart dismissed this subject with a snort. "Magicians! There was a time you wouldn't have found his kind on a ship like this."

"A magician." Mehitabel shook her head. "Fancy that."

Haywood Cathcart did not choose to respond. Instead, he smiled at his somber-faced daughter. "I want you to take good care of yourself, pet. You're the only one we have left."

"I will, Father," Millicent said quietly.

"And give my regards to your mother. I've written to her, of course, and she will be expecting both of you. No doubt she and Gregory"—he said this name with a mixture of contempt and anger—"will meet you in Genoa."

"They have before," Millicent said, disliking this part of their farewells. She had to endure them every year, and every year she felt more awkward.

"I've given my sister enough pin money for the voyage, and my bank authorization is waiting for you in Geneva. If there are any unexpected expenses, the Captain has my authorization to spend whatever is necessary." He gave her a jovial grin. "The Briarcliff is a wonderful automobile, isn't it? Much nicer than the Adams, although I should have come in the Brescia Bugatti—it's the newest. I'm so afraid that it will get dented in all the crush." Haywood Cathcart was an enthusiastic automobilist, and once he started on his favorite subject was likely to continue for some time. He restrained himself now, adding only, "I'm hoping to order a Daimler tourer. You can ride in it next summer, pet."

"That will be nice, Father," said Millicent, thinking that to her one automobile was very much like another, except for the very fast and low-slung Italia that Gregory drove some of the time.

"I'll have you know we went forty-five miles an hour in the Briarcliff," Haywood Cathcart boasted.

"So fast!" Mehitabel said, one shapely gloved hand pressed to her bosom. "Haywood, you mustn't."

"It's exciting," said Haywood Cathcart, and then reluctantly changed the subject. "I've looked over the list of first-class passengers, pet, and there's no one you need avoid, not with your Aunt Mehitabel along to look after you. High time you let her come with you on this trip." He winked at his daughter, trying to make her see the humor he felt in the situation. "Your mother's sister was with you last year, and before that you had Nanny. In a few more years, you'll probably try to talk me into letting you travel with one of your cousins instead of your Aunt Mehitabel."

"I shouldn't think so, Father," said Millicent, who hardly knew her cousins.

"Why, Haywood," protested Mehitabel, "don't put such ideas in the child's head."

"It's a new century, Mehitabel, and a decade's gone by already. They say there'll be more automobiles than carriages by nineteen twenty." His expression was hopeful.

"Haywood, that's ridiculous," Mehitabel rebuked him. "Stop teasing. Just because you're so keen on automobiles and heaven alone knows what else, you think that the whole world is like you." She tried to sound stern and succeeded only in pouting.

"You wait and see," Haywood Cathcart insisted, then tried again with his daughter. "I want you to write to me as soon as you reach Genoa, and tell me that you're safe and sound. You're precious to me, pet. You know you are."

"Yes, Father." She fiddled with her hat, trying to make it rest properly on her light brown ringlets.

"I haven't any chick or child left but you," he continued, as he always did when she was about to leave.

"Yes, Father." Millicent sighed and stood while he kissed her on the cheek, then gave him a single, efficient kiss above the curl of his moustache. "God bless, Father."

"And keep you, Millicent," he said as seriously as he ever said anything to her. "You listen to Aunt Mehitabel and do as she tells you. Remember, she's as much your parent as either your mother or I while you're traveling."

"I will, Father." She stepped back, feeling self-conscious. Her father often confused her, and never more than when he was saying good-bye; he paid more attention to her for those few minutes than for all her summer visit.

Haywood Cathcart gave a hearty farewell to his sister, then waved at his daughter, already leaving the deck. "I'll see you next June, pet," he called out to Millicent before he was lost to sight among the others thronging toward the gangway leading back to the dock.

Mehitabel wiped a tear from the corner of her eye. "He's always so thoughtful. Such a generous man."

"Did he give you a fifty-dollar gold piece?" Millicent asked shrewdly.

"Yes," Mehitabel said, astonished at Millicent's question.

"He always does that, no matter who's traveling with me," Millicent said in her self-possessed way. "He gives out a gold piece 'just in case,' and then leaves." She looked down at the dock, toward the Briarcliff. "Do you think," she ventured to ask her aunt as she watched for her father in the mob, "that he is going to marry Corrine, or is she just another invisible woman in his life?"

"Millicent!" hissed Mehitabel, very much shocked. "How do you know about . . . Corrine?"

"Father always has an invisible woman, doesn't he? The way that Mama has Gregory, though Father doesn't admit it." She paused and then, when her aunt did not reprimand her for the observation, she went on. "Father used to keep—that's the word, isn't it?"

"Yes," admitted a distressed Mehitabel, "*not* that you should know such things, because you shouldn't, miss."

"Well, Father used to keep a pretty woman named Jenny, but last year she was gone and there was no one. Corrine isn't like the others. Her father's well-to-do, and that's not the same, is it?"

"I don't know anything about it," said Mehitabel, then, in relief, she pointed. "There's Haywood. Wave to him, Millicent."

Obediently Millicent waved to her father and kept her thoughts to herself.

2

Adjoining the main dining room was a Grand Salon, fitted out with a long, polished bar at one end, and with a number of small tables and settees where the first-class passengers could gather before being seated for meals.

Mehitabel had donned her second most impressive gown for that first evening out—she was saving the most impressive for their last evening aboard—and now had taken her place on one of the settees, Millicent beside her in a high-necked, tuck-fronted linen frock proper for a girl her age. "You look very pretty, Millicent," Mehitabel whispered to her, plucking the ends of her sash so that they hung in a more attractive line. "Do sit up straight."

"I am sitting up straight, Aunt Mehitabel," she said in her quiet way. "The settee has too wide a seat for me."

"Then put your feet on the floor and keep your back forward," her aunt instructed her, and fixed a sociable smile on her lips. "Who do you suppose that man in the uniform is? He looks foreign."

The impressive officer in question stood between the settee where Mehitabel and Millicent sat and the bar. His tunic was grand with gold braid and medals. He had a small, very neat moustache over an even smaller mouth, dark, discontented eyes; and a profusion of glossy dark hair starting to gray at the temples. He approached the bar and addressed the waiter there in a harsh voice.

"Is that French?" Mehitabel asked of no one in particular.

"It's Spanish," Millicent said. "I believe he said that he's a General, but I'm not sure. I don't speak Spanish, only Italian and French."

"How fortunate," murmured Mehitabel. "It's your European education."

"I'm supposed to learn German this year." Millicent sighed. "Miss Nachbar is the German teacher."

"How nice," said Mehitabel, watching the Spanish General as if he were an animal she thought could be dangerous.

A young couple entered the lounge, both well dressed and rosy, each watching the other with the sort of adoration that proclaimed them newly married. The woman was giggling at something her husband had whispered to her. "Jared, not here."

He added something else, and she blushed. They went to the bar and stood some distance from the Spaniard.

Another couple arrived, this one less happily than the first. The man was white-haired and bent, sitting in a wheeled chair with a woolen lap robe spread over his legs.

Accompanying the chief steward, who pushed the chair, was a tall, angular woman of middle age, dressed in a flowing gown of lilac satin with pale lace insets at the bosom. Two tall egret feathers rose above her lavish coiffure.

"What an elegant woman," Mehitabel said to Millicent, watching the newcomers with great interest. "How unfortunate that her husband is an invalid."

"Are you sure he is her husband?" asked Millicent.

"I suppose he is. Who else would she be traveling with under these circumstances?" Aunt Mehitabel was not the sort of woman who could glare at anyone, but she could express disapproval in the tone of her voice, and she did so now.

"Oh, her brother, or a cousin," Millicent suggested innocently.

"No doubt the Captain will inform us of their relationship when we go in to dine," Mehitabel said in quelling accents.

"Waiter," said the woman in lilac, "I would like a sherry for myself and your best mineral water for Mister Dovecote."

"At once," said the nearest waiter, watching as the chief steward maneuvered the wheeled chair to one of the small tables.

"Thank you," said the woman, handing a coin to the chief steward.

"Thank *you*, Missus Dovecote," said the chief steward in heavily accented English.

A number of other passengers were gathering in the Grand Salon, arriving in a rush now that it was half an hour before the first dinner seating. It was the traditional time for sherry, and this first night out, all the passengers appeared to be curious about their fellows.

"There's that pleasant Mister Wingham," said Mehitabel as the gentleman in question walked up to the bar. He was in formal clothes, as were all the others except the invalid. He looked around and smiled at Mehitabel in a friendly way before turning to the thin, nervous man at his side.

There was another arrival, and this one created a moment of surprised silence: a young woman in a severely plain evening dress, a simple pearl necklace, and no other trace of jewelry came into the Grand Salon by herself. She gave the entire gathering a quick, challenging look, then walked directly to the bar and ordered a sherry. Conversation resumed at once, too loudly.

"What effrontery," Mehitabel declared, but not much above a whisper. "Look at her!"

"I think she's a sensible woman," Millicent said to her aunt.

"But to come in alone like that . . . and to order sherry . . ." Mehitabel toyed with the largest of her jeweled bracelets. "It's scandalous."

"She's very brave," Millicent decided aloud.

"Brazen, you mean." Mehitabel sniffed. "Unescorted, and flaunting it."

"Not every woman can be escorted, Aunt," Millicent pointed out, rather sadly; she wondered if she would ever be squired that way.

"On a ship of this sort, it is proper for her to be escorted, young lady," Mehitabel insisted.

"Still," Millicent said, and did not go on, for she saw that Geoffrey Wingham was coming toward them, carrying his glass of sherry and smiling.

"Missus Reyns," he said in his charming way, "and your niece, Miss Cathcart. How good to see you again. It's pleasant to learn that we share the first seating for dinner."

"Good evening, Mister Wingham," said Mehitabel, at her most gracious. "Perhaps you would care to join us for a few minutes."

"How kind," he said, taking the chair next to the settee. "I was talking to the first officer not more than twenty minutes ago, and he told me that they are expecting to enter a storm some time tomorrow."

"Goodness!" said Mehitabel. "A storm at sea; it must be frightening."

"He assured me that we should not encounter heavy weather after that. Marvelous expression, isn't it: 'heavy weather,' as if it were a burden." He had the sort of smile that made his eyes narrow and crinkle, the sort of smile that made him look both younger and older than he was.

"I've been in storms before," Millicent said, although neither adult paid her much attention. She folded her hands and let her eyes wander about the room while her aunt talked with Mister Wingham.

One man caught her attention; he was tall and lean, with golden-brown hair swept back from his brow. His eyes were the same golden-brown as his hair and a bit sunken; his nose was lean and tending to the aquiline. He held a long, thin cheroot between his fingers, and he did not mingle with the passengers around him. Millicent thought she knew exactly the way he felt.

"And you, Millicent," Mehitabel said emphatically, recalling her to her surroundings. "You must thank Mister Wingham for his kind offer."

"Oh?" Millicent said, blinking once. "Thank you, Mister Wingham."

"Your niece has lovely manners," Mister Wingham said to Mehitabel, as if Millicent herself could not hear him.

"Why, thank you," said Mehitabel, and Millicent once again stopped listening. She once again let her eyes roam over the other passengers, and she tried to guess something about each one. The little, nervous man in the dinner jacket with the satin lapels was probably a lawyer or an official of some sort, traveling for the government or an important businessman, because there was no reason such an inconspicuous and awkward man should be booked into first-class accommodations otherwise. The three older ladies with the jeweled necklaces and very expensive clothes Millicent decided were sisters, probably widows sharing their prosperity and their grief. Four diverse couples other than the newlyweds were seated at the little tables, and Millicent was certain she had heard one of them speaking German or perhaps Swedish.

"Ladies and gentlemen," said the chief steward from the door to the dining room, "if you will be kind enough to step this way, we will seat you for the first serving." His accent was strange to Millicent, but she had to admit that his English was quite good in spite of the accent.

"Come, Millicent," said Aunt Mehitabel as she rose. "It was good of you to spare us so much of your time," she told Mister Wingham.

"I hope that we will have other opportunities to speak again, Missus Reyns," he said gallantly, withdrawing without fuss and returning to the bar to leave his glass before entering the dining room.

"You are invited to join the Captain at his table," said the chief steward when Mehitabel identified herself and Millicent.

"How wonderful," said Mehitabel, adding to Millicent, "isn't it wonderful, dear?"

"Father usually arranges for me to eat at the Captain's table the first night out," Millicent said softly, feeling embarrassed by her aunt's gushiness.

"That's so good of Haywood. I'm so grateful to him for everything he's done for me. You must feel it yourself," Mehitabel went on as they made their way through the huge, ornate room to the long Captain's table. "Oh, heavens. You're on the Captain's right," she cried to Millicent.

"That's good," Millicent said, wishing that she were by herself, like the young woman in the simple gown, or that her aunt might be struck silent for ten minutes.

A few minutes later they were joined by the tall man Millicent had been watching earlier. He bowed to each of them and said, "Good evening, ladies," before he took his seat on the Captain's left, facing Millicent.

The Spanish General was next to arrive, and he all but clicked his heels before taking his seat at the far end of the table. Two more diners arrived as the Captain himself came to the table.

"Good evening," he said affably. "I am Captain Symington, and it is my pleasure to welcome you all aboard the *Duchess of Malfi*. I trust we will all have a most enjoyable crossing." With that as an introduction, he sat down and offered his hand first to Millicent, saying, "It's good to see you again, little lady. You've grown up some since I saw you last year."

"It's good of you to notice, Captain," said Mehitabel for Millicent. "Her father remarked on the same thing."

"He's a lucky man to have such a pretty daughter," said Captain Symington. "And you must be his sister, Missus Reyns."

"Yes," said Mehitabel, holding out her hand.

Millicent stared hard at her water glass, then looked up quickly to see the man opposite her give her a brief, understanding smile.

The Spaniard turned out to be General Enrique Esteban Hernán María Martín Luis Vicente Cuernos y Arreba, returning to Spain from Cuba. He accepted the Captain's welcome as his due and looked around the table as if he had been seated with trained dogs. "It is an honor," he said, as if he meant that it was the others, not himself, who were honored.

The last introduction was saved for the man opposite Millicent, and the Captain was plainly saving what he felt to be the best for last.

"As most of you have heard by now, we have the privilege to be taking the company of the Incredible Anton back to Europe after his triumphant three-year tour of the United States of America. For your entertainment, the Incredible Anton has promised to perform many of his fascinating miracles for us during the crossing, conditions permitting. I know we will all be delighted with your performances, sir," the Captain finished as he turned to the tall man.

The Incredible Anton met Millicent's surprised eyes with

an expression of almost lazy amusement. Slowly he stood up and looked over the passengers seated with him. "I am delighted to meet you all and only regret that I must limit my performances during this voyage. However, if our entertainments please you, my troupe and I will be handsomely rewarded." He smiled and sat down once more.

Millicent, listening to him with care, decided that although his English was excellent, it was excellent in the same way her French was, and that he had learned it well, but not as his first language.

"I understand that we are to have a choice of two soups, one of them cold because of the weather," the Captain said in order to get the proper table conversation under way. Then he turned to Anton and said with great cordiality, "I am very pleased you agreed to perform for the passengers. It will make this crossing memorable for all of us."

Anton shrugged slightly. "It is a very good way for all of my troupe to stay in practice. I appreciate the opportunity you're giving us."

Millicent listened with great interest, her curiosity undisguised, and Captain Symington noticed.

"You're going to be amazed, Miss Cathcart. I've seen the Incredible Anton perform, and he baffled me completely. No doubt you'll be dazzled by his feats."

Before Millicent could think of a response, Anton himself spoke up. "I would be surprised if there is much that dazzles this young lady."

Although she tried very hard not to blush, Millicent could feel the heat in her face and knew she had turned scarlet. This made her feel more awkward than ever, but she did her best to sound composed even if she did not look that way. "I like surprises, Mister Anton; I like to figure them out, as well."

He chuckled. "Not Mister Anton, simply Anton, which is my given name, not my surname."

Millicent had rarely called any adult by his first name, and it made her feel strangely grown-up to address him by his. "Anton, if that is what you prefer."

The waiter arrived with the first of the two soups, a cold consommé served with cream floating on it.

"This looks superb, Captain Symington," Mehitabel said, and nudged Millicent with her elbow.

"Yes," Millicent said, in answer to her aunt's prodding, "superb."

3

By morning the storm that had grumbled in the distance for most of the night caught up with the *Duchess of Malfi*. Many of the passengers elected to remain in their cabins while the huge white ship plowed through the roiling seas. The air was colder, and light coats came out of trunks to keep the travelers warm.

"I ought not to have had the squab," moaned Mehitabel as she huddled in her bed. "I will call for one of the understewards to accompany you to the dining room if you insist on eating anything."

"I can find my way, Aunt," Millicent said. "There won't be many persons in the dining room. There never are when the seas are high like this."

"How can you bear it?" Mehitabel demanded, then held her hand to her mouth as she stumbled toward the door to the bathroom.

Millicent felt sympathy for her aunt, but knew that there was nothing she could do to alleviate her seasickness. She took her coat and pulled it on, calling out, "I'll ask one of the understewards to bring you something to make you feel better."

"Don't talk to anyone," Mehitabel managed to warn her.

"I'll be careful," Millicent promised, confident that this was answer enough and was honest, for she hoped to have some conversation.

Once in the hallway that led toward the Grand Salon and the dining room, Millicent took care to hang on to the polished brass railings that ran along one wall, for there was enough roll to the ship to make progress tricky, but not too difficult. Millicent caught herself humming, which she had done as a child when she wanted to give herself courage. She smiled, for much the same reason.

In the Grand Salon, she found the self-sufficient young woman who had so shocked the passengers the night before. She was sitting at one of the small tables, dressed in expensive but simple clothes, her traveling suit of heavy tan linen unrelieved by lace or bows. It was clear that she was not, as she had the evening before, confining her figure with corsets. She looked up at Millicent, saying, "Hello," in a pleasant voice.

"Hello," Millicent answered, taking the chair across from her. "My name is Millicent Cathcart. What's your name, please?"

The young woman did not smile, but her manner softened. "I am Miss Gordon, Cloris Gordon." She paused, then added, "I am traveling to France to continue my education."

"I'm going back to school in Switzerland," Millicent told her, as if this would assure their understanding.

"A finishing school?" Miss Cloris Gordon asked with faint contempt.

"I don't really know," Millicent answered seriously. "They expect us to learn a great deal, and they make sure we know how to behave politely. Is that a finishing school?"

"Do you study the sciences and mathematics as well as learn how to be polite?" Before Millicent could reply, Miss Gordon went on, "I am an educationalist. It is shameful that we as a society routinely refuse to educate women while we equally routinely force education on men who are ill prepared to use it."

"I have a botany teacher and a mathematics teacher at the school," Millicent said, deciding to answer Miss Gordon's question. "Two of the other girls were taking a tutorial in biology last term."

"That's something," Miss Gordon said grudgingly. "Is your mother still in her cabin?"

"My mother is in Geneva; I am traveling with my paternal aunt," said Millicent, looking toward the dining room door and wishing it would open.

"I see," said Miss Gordon, then followed her glance. "They're late serving this morning. Apparently one of the waiters is ill." She looked up as the hall door opened once again and the nervous man she had seen with Mister Wingham came into the room. He took a place as far away from Millicent and Miss Cloris Gordon as possible and resolutely turned his face toward the rain-spattered window.

"Who is he, do you know?" Millicent asked in an undervoice.

"His name is Milton Homes. I understand he is a professor, but he has not been willing to disclose his area of study to me," answered Miss Gordon with a disapproving edge to her voice.

"He reminds me of a rabbit. I expect his nose to twitch," Millicent remarked, trying to speak softly so that she would not offend the innocuous Mister—or Professor—Milton Homes.

This observation startled Miss Gordon, who blinked once at Millicent before she spoke. "You're a most imaginative young woman."

"Oh, I don't think so," Millicent said. "I'm much too sensible, or so my teachers tell me. Besides, it doesn't take any imagination to think that gentleman looks like a rabbit. If he were more forceful," she added thoughtfully, "I might almost say a ferret."

The door to the dining room was thrown open and the chief steward stepped through it. "We of the *Duchess of Malfi* apologize for the delay in serving breakfast. If you would be kind enough to take your seats, our waiters will attend to you at once." Again his accent sounded heavily with the English words.

"Where does he come from?" Millicent wondered aloud.

"Somewhere in the Balkans, I should think," said Miss Gordon as she rose. "He has the look about him, and the accent certainly isn't German."

"No, not German," Millicent agreed, thinking of her approaching German classes.

"It's an interesting accent, I will agree," Miss Gordon said, as if to encourage Millicent in some way. "You are not unintelligent."

"Yes, I know," said Millicent, and found that Miss Gordon was not pleased by her admission. "My teachers have said so."

"It does not become you to be too proud at this stage in your education," Miss Gordon cautioned Millicent before she went to her table.

Millicent said nothing more, but went to her table and waited for her breakfast.

Afterward, Millicent wandered about the first-class deck, pausing in the doorway of the Grand Salon, where three men, including the Spanish General, were playing cards with a large number of chips in front of them. When they noticed her, they scowled, and the General said a few terse words in Spanish: Millicent did not need to understand them to know she was being ordered to depart. She thought about returning to her cabin, but knew that Aunt Mehitabel would not welcome her company. Finally she reached the Grand Ballroom and noticed that the tall, carved, and glossy wooden doors were ajar. She hesitated, then, hearing a voice, stepped into the room.

The windows at the far end of the ballroom were covered with solid wooden shutters, and so the huge chamber was nearly dark, its three enormous chandeliers shrouded in dust covers, like the tops of enormous, trunkless trees. At the other end of the room, two men were laboring in the wan light of a single sconce bulb to build an extension on the low stage where the orchestra usually played. It took Millicent a moment to recognize the taller of the two as the Incredible Anton. She stepped farther into the room, her curiosity increasing.

The man working with the Incredible Anton turned around suddenly, his swarthy features fixed in an angry grimace. He held a hammer in his hand.

Millicent stopped, more frightened than she cared to admit.

The Incredible Anton put down the screwdriver he held and rose, looking down at Millicent. "Miss Cathcart, isn't it?"

"Yes," Millicent answered, pleased that she did not sound scared.

"I'm glad to see that the storm hasn't driven you to your cabin the way it has so many of the passengers. You can put that hammer away, Jibben. Miss Cathcart isn't going to make off with any of my things." He looked back at Millicent. "We're improvising, since we need a bigger stage than what is available, and proper wings." He indicated the half-finished proscenium arch he and his assistant were building. "Luckily we've had to improvise before and came equipped."

"Are you going to perform here, then?" Millicent asked.

"Tomorrow night, I hope, weather permitting," Anton answered. "The Captain assures me that we'll be through the worst of this by nightfall. That will give me some time to develop alternate illusions. I hope he's right."

Jibben ignored Millicent, speaking to Anton as if no one else were with them. "Do you want me to keep on with this?"

"Certainly," Anton told him, then once again gave his attention to Millicent. "Miss Cathcart, if you like, I'll show you what we're doing here."

"Yes, I'd like that very much." She did her best to be polite, but she was too interested to turn down his offer, though she knew it was what she ought to do. "I'm fascinated."

Anton did not appear to mind. "Well, it should be obvious that when we're through, we'll have a small stage here. You can see there is no room for trapdoors in the floor, and though there is a high ceiling in this room, we can't rig the flies—that is, the overhead curtains—to hang from the ceiling. I asked Captain Symington about that before we sailed, and he said it would not be possible. That limits some of the illusions we can perform here, as does the roll of the ship. Stage magic is often very delicate."

"You're telling her too much," Jibben grumbled. His accent was vaguely English, but with an odd flavor to it, and he seemed to be indifferent to his surroundings.

"Oh, I don't think so. Miss Cathcart—or may I call you Millicent?—isn't the sort of child who spends all her time looking for wonders; she spends all her time looking for reasons. Am I right?"

Millicent stared at the Incredible Anton in amazement. In all her fourteen years, no one had ever recognized that aspect of her nature, which she considered to be the core of herself. "Reasons are the heart of everything, aren't they?"

Anton smiled and nodded. "You see, Jibben? We have nothing to fear from Miss Cathcart."

"Millicent," she said, feeling very grown-up indeed.

"But I trust that when you find the reasons for the illusions we perform, you will not tell everyone what you have discovered." He paused, as if to continue, then changed his mind. "Can you tell me why I say this?"

Millicent cocked her head to the side and gave his question her serious consideration. "First, the secret and the . . . illusions are yours. Second, I might be wrong, and that would make everyone, including me, feel foolish." She stopped, but saw that he was still waiting. "Is there something more?"

Anton laughed. "In many ways, the most important reason of all, though you may not believe it. Most of the persons in our audience don't *want* to know how the illusions are done—they would rather have the mysteries than the truth."

"Really?" Millicent asked, clearly unconvinced.

"Oh, yes, I promise you. Most of the persons on board this ship would prefer to be fooled than to know the truth. You are the exception, no matter what the others would say if you asked them. I know this. It's my work to know it." He looked up as one of the understewards came into the ballroom, saying to the man, "May I be of help?"

The understeward was visibly upset and he hesitated, not knowing what to say. "Excuse me. I forgot you were in here." He started out of the door, but stopped. "You have not seen another understeward here, have you?"

"Not since early this morning," Anton told him. "Jibben, have you seen one of the understewards since we began setting up in here?"

Jibben shook his head. "They've left us alone until now."

"Is there some trouble?" Anton inquired with concern.

"I hope not," the understeward said; going on reluctantly, he explained, "One of the understewards is missing. We've been trying to find him, but he doesn't appear to be on board. . . ."

"And you fear he might have come to some harm?" Anton suggested gently.

"In this storm, it could happen," the understeward said, his face looking suddenly old.

"I hope you will be proven mistaken," said Anton, and turned to Jibben. "What about Sabina?"

"She's still in her cabin," said Jibben scornfully. "She gets seasick."

"Sadly true," said Anton, then looked at the understeward attentively. "I'm sorry we can't be of more help."

"What you've done is appreciated," the understeward said, adding anxiously, "Don't mention this, if you would. We don't want to distress the passengers, and news of this sort always seems to upset them. They don't understand that they're better taken care of than some of us are." He started to pull the door closed, then said, "It's probably a mistake, in any case. He's probably overslept or has found a dicing game with the engineers."

"It's possible," Anton allowed as the understeward left. "Poor man," he added when the understeward was gone.

"Do you think the other one fell overboard?" Millicent asked, very intrigued.

"I don't know—what matters is that *he,* the other understeward, thinks that he has, and it worries him." He shook his head. "It's time I was getting back to work. I can't leave it all to Jibben."

Millicent knew that he was sending her away, and although she would have preferred to remain and watch, she realized there was nothing to gain in arguing with the magician. "Thank you for showing me as much as you did. I'm looking forward to your performance, and I give you my word that if I have any theories about your . . . illusions, I will discuss them only with you."

"Good girl," the Incredible Anton said. Then, in a different tone, he warned her, "Don't mention that understeward, Millicent. Rumors on board a ship can be very dangerous."

"I won't," she promised, and went out the door of the Grand Ballroom, satisfied that her morning had not been wasted.

4

"Did you hear? One of the understewards was washed overboard during the storm," Aunt Mehitabel informed Millicent in shocked accents as the two of them dressed for dinner that night.

"Really?" Millicent said, proud of herself for sounding so indifferent to the news.

"It's a terrible thing. What a dreadful way to die!" Mehitabel dusted her bosom with scented powder and looked in the mirror with a critical expression. "Oh, dear, I wish I weren't so wan. I'm looking quite hagged."

"It's because you've been seasick, and there's nothing strange about that," Millicent said, attempting to show sympathy openly.

"The seasickness was bad enough, but it's left me looking so dreadful, I shrink at the thought of going in to dinner. What will people think?"

"Many of them will look just the same way, Aunt," Millicent reminded her, then said, "Most of them will feel for you."

"I do hope you're right," Mehitabel declared as she tried to finish fastening her gown. "Can you help me with this, dear?"

"All right," Millicent said, going to fasten the hooks and eyes up the back of Mehitabel's dress.

"I told Haywood that it would be more convenient to have a maid with us, but since there are two waiting in Europe, he said that we could manage for the voyage. Men do not understand what women have to go through, or they would not be so indifferent to our difficulties. I understand the problem of expense, but it is very awkward at moments like this to . . ." She stopped while she looked in the mirror and adjusted the reembroidered lace that reached to her throat. "Do you think that this fits properly here, Millicent?"

Millicent dutifully inspected the beautifully made dress and said, "It is magnificent, Aunt, and so are you, even if you think you're not."

"You can see that I'm not." Mehitabel sighed. "Let me warn you now, Millicent, never be a widow. It is very hard."

"I don't think that will be my decision to make," Millicent said seriously.

Mehitabel blinked. "Well, no, I suppose not. But you know what I mean by this, surely?" She glanced at her niece in the mirror. "Perhaps you don't. I must have a talk with your mother when I see her."

"The teachers at my school have told us about human reproduction, if that's what you mean," Millicent said, trying to be very nonchalant about having this information.

"Have they? Goodness gracious! Do your parents know about this? Does your mother approve?" Before Millicent could answer, Mehitabel commented darkly, "Not that one can approve of your mother, though she is a dear."

Millicent's hands became still and she asked in a soft voice, "What do you mean?"

"Well," Mehitabel said, feeling very awkward now, "I suppose you've discussed this with your father."

"I don't talk about Mother with Father or Father with Mother if I can help it," Millicent said, more quietly than ever. "And I try not to talk about either of them to anyone else."

"Oh," Mehitabel said, clearly distressed now. "I didn't realize. From what Haywood said, I thought you understood about your mother."

"I understand she does not wish to live with my father and that they are not able to divorce," Millicent said flatly. "I also understand that my mother lives with Gregory and that this year my father is sleeping with but not living with a woman named Corrine. I may be only fourteen, but I'm not so young that I don't know these things, Aunt." She had learned over the years to hide her emotions about her parents, but as always, when she talked about them, there was a coldness within her, and a loneliness.

"It's really most unfortunate," Mehitabel said a bit later. Her silence had become worse than speech would be.

"I think so," Millicent said, and did not explain or offer to explain.

Mehitabel tittered uneasily. "Dear me, we might be late to sherry if you don't hurry. Are you going to wear that periwinkle silk tonight, or the linen?"

"I think I'll wear the sprigged muslin. It's not too cool for a summer dinner dress, is it?" She liked the pale green sprigged muslin with the wide sash that crossed her hips. It had a square neck and an enormous number of pin tucks running from the neckline to the dropped waist, and triple-layer pleats beneath.

"It's very becoming," Mehitabel said as she reached for her vial of perfume. "But hurry. It's almost time for sherry."

The evening sky was filled with the hot colors of sunset and long, festive streamers of clouds, the last of the storm following the main body, like party makers following a parade. The wind was chilly, but once they entered the Grand Salon, it was warm enough.

Miss Gordon was sitting by herself near the window, and Millicent made a point of greeting her. "Good evening," she said, then went on—to Mehitabel's outrage—to say, "This is my aunt, Missus Reyns."

"A pleasure, I'm sure," Mehitabel said in her chilliest voice.

"I am Miss Gordon," the other said as cordially as Mehitabel.

"Miss Gordon is going to Europe to continue her studies," Millicent informed her aunt, who bristled at the news. "I think it's wonderful."

"I feel that the education of women is sadly lacking," Miss Gordon declared, making it a general challenge to the whole room.

"Women? Educated?" General Cuernos responded from his place by the bar. Unlike the others, he was having whiskey this evening.

"It is one of the most pressing social issues," Miss Gordon declared. "For only when women are educated will it be possible for them to be able to vote and hold public office competently. Although no such competence is demanded of men."

"My dear young, and if I may say so, foolish woman,"

the General said as he turned to give her the benefit of an amused and contemptuous laugh, "the world will have come to a sorry pass if women are ever granted the vote. If women were capable of such judgments, such enfranchisement would have happened long ago, for men of honor would have insisted." He shrugged eloquently. "As we are aware, such has not happened."

"Then we must assume," Miss Gordon said loudly, "that men of honor are fewer than previously supposed."

"For heaven's sake . . ." Mehitabel whispered to Millicent. "Don't linger."

"My aunt wishes to sit down, Miss Gordon. We'll talk later." Millicent could not understand why she found this encounter so stimulating, but she felt herself thrilled by the clash between Miss Gordon and the General. She smiled at Miss Gordon and then followed Mehitabel to a table on the far side of the Grand Salon.

"I want you never to make such a spectacle of yourself again, miss," Mehitabel told her in a furious undervoice. "It's beyond all bounds, your behavior."

"But, Aunt—" Millicent protested.

"Not another word on the subject." She held up her gloved hand, then set about the business of unfastening the six pearl buttons at her wrist and tugging the tight-fitting kid off her hand.

"May I have the privilege of bringing you a sherry, Missus Reyns?" said Geoffrey Wingham as he approached Mehitabel and Millicent. "Have you heard about the missing understeward? Shocking."

"Oh, yes," Mehitabel said gratefully. "I was very distressed to learn of it, and you are very kind to offer sherry, to say nothing of helping us avoid unpleasantness." She nodded significantly in the direction of Miss Gordon.

"I hope you will not be troubled again," came his gallant response. "No doubt each has a valid point, but it is not for the likes of us, or even for them, it would seem, to resolve so complex a matter." He smiled winningly at Mehitabel and then at Millicent, saying, "Would you like a seltzered drink?"

Millicent looked to her aunt, and saw a slight nod. "That's very kind. Orgeat would be nice."

"Orgeat. How very European." He chuckled as he strolled away to the bar to get the sherry and the seltzered orgeat for Millicent.

"He's a most accommodating man," Mehitabel said, watching him go.

"Yes," Millicent agreed, and wondered what it was about Mister Wingham that she did not like.

"I see that Mister and Missus Dovecote are here," Mehitabel said, continuing with the polite conversation she had been taught to make many years ago. "It is unfortunate that he should be an invalid."

"Yes," Millicent said, feeling terribly bored.

"I must speak with her, I think. We are much the same age and no doubt we will have much in common." She looked up, smiling warmly, as Mister Wingham returned carrying two glasses.

"They're planning to serve the dinner promptly this evening. From what the bartender had to say, the loss of the understeward has been inconvenient, but not too dreadful for his department." He sat down across from Mehitabel and proceeded to make himself agreeable to her.

Millicent's attention wandered as she sipped her almond-flavored drink. She wanted to continue her conversation with Miss Gordon but knew that her aunt would not permit it, so she let her eyes drift from one passenger to another. She noticed that Mister Homes was in the most remote corner of the room, and she thought that, like some of the shy people she knew, he appeared to be hiding. How sad that he should be an adult and still behave like a child. Then she saw that the Incredible Anton had come into the Grand Salon, and she gave him an ungenteel little wave. She felt after her conversation with him that she was not taking liberties.

Apparently he thought so, too, for he raised his hand enough to assure her he was waving, and then gave his attention to the elderly French couple near him.

"That's not polite, Millicent," Mehitabel reminded her, seeing the exchange.

"I talked to him before, Aunt Mehitabel. And Captain Symington introduced us." It was delightful to say these things to her aunt, since it was one way she could show her independence without defiance and without self-aggrandizement.

"The man's an entertainer," Mehitabel reminded her, as if this explained something.

"He is supposed to be very good. I hope he is," Millicent said, not letting Mehitabel fluster her. "I'm so glad that he's on the voyage. Most crossings are boring without entertainment, and I'm not old enough to dance yet."

"Very true," Geoffrey Wingham said, showing sympathy for her plight. "A child on a crossing like this must be hard put to pass the time."

"Her father wants her to begin her school studies," Mehitabel said with a trace of severity.

"I have been reading Mister Dickens's novel *Bleak House,*

and some of the stories of Mister Kipling. Miss Viederbaum, who teaches literature, is very keen on Kipling." Millicent took pleasure in saying this because she knew that Mehitabel did not read many books, preferring when she did what Haywood Cathcart called "improving essays," such as those of Mister Emerson.

"Very erudite for so young a lady," Mister Wingham said with a kindly expression that made Millicent long to throw something at him.

"Say thank you, Millicent," Mehitabel coaxed her.

"Thank you," Millicent said, biting off the two words.

"They say that the Incredible Anton is going to do a short program after dinner," Mister Wingham went on. "I'm looking forward to it, aren't you?"

"Yes, goodness yes," Mehitabel enthused, taking a cautious sip of her sherry. Her hesitance with the fortified wine came from her concern that her seasickness might not be entirely over, and she dreaded making any sort of scene. "I hear that he is quite remarkable."

"He has an international reputation," Mister Wingham stated, as if this guaranteed a better evening than if the Incredible Anton were wholly unknown.

The chief steward appeared and announced that the first seating was about to begin, and those waiting in the lounge rose and went into the dining room.

Two hours later, Captain Symington informed those who were selecting their desserts that in half an hour there would be a display of magic and legerdemain in the Grand Ballroom, an announcement that was met with scattered applause. Hearing this, the Incredible Anton rose to his feet and gave a short bow.

"I hope," he said mellifluously, "that you will enjoy

what my troupe and I perform for you. This is only a sample of the wonders we will bring to you during the voyage, of course."

"I think he's a very odd man," Mehitabel said softly to Millicent when they were seated in the Ballroom. "It's one thing to know a few card tricks, but something else to transform handkerchiefs into rose trees. I understand he's done that."

"They say that he has a great talent," Mister Wingham said, doing his best to make it clear that he was in complete agreement with Mehitabel. "Missus Reyns, surely you don't think that he can actually *do* the things he appears to do?"

"I haven't had the pleasure of seeing him perform," she said, which was not an answer.

"Well, in a little while . . ." He nodded as the lights dimmed and the curtains of the makeshift stage parted. "There."

"Good evening," the Incredible Anton said, addressing his audience, holding out his arms in a gesture of welcome. In the next moment there was a long cane in his right hand. "It is a pleasure to greet you all. You have been good enough to come here for wonders, and wonders you shall have." He gestured with the cane, and it was instantly transformed into a handful of silken scarves.

There was a scattering of applause and the Incredible Anton acknowledged it graciously.

"How does he do that?" Millicent whispered to her aunt.

"I can't imagine," Mehitabel answered, her mouth a little open in astonishment.

The Incredible Anton was continuing, gathering up the silks into his hand, then tapping his knuckles.

"Most things are not what they seem to be, are they?" he asked urbanely as he opened his hand to reveal an egg where the silken scarves had been. "I will now perform for you, since I have one of the necessary ingredients, a very ancient Chinese illusion called *hai don ton doi,* the 'Egg in the Bag.' " And he produced a small, flat velvet bag. "You see, here is the egg"—he held it up so that the audience could see it clearly—"and I put it into the bag so." He placed the egg in the bag, then strolled to the edge of the stage and proceeded to tap the bag three times on the proscenium arch. There was an intake of breath in the audience, as everyone anticipated the cracking of the egg. It did not happen. The bag appeared to be flat and empty. The Incredible Anton tapped the bag again, then turned it inside out and repeated the taps. "As you see, the egg has disappeared, but . . ." He made a pass over the bag and held it up, the top of it open, and he said, "The egg will return." He took the bag in his hands, pressed it, and the egg emerged once more. He held it up, and bowed to acknowledge the applause.

Of the nine tricks—illusions—the Incredible Anton performed that night, Millicent liked the floating ball best, in which the Incredible Anton made a large metallic ball waft through the air by gestures of his hands.

As the magician took his final bow, he caught Millicent's eye for a moment, and there was an amused challenge in his face.

5

"It was most remarkable," Mehitabel was still declaring by lunchtime the following day.

"Are you speaking of the Incredible Anton?" asked Auralia Dovecote, who had apparently left her invalid husband with his attendant and was taking time to enjoy a meal on her own.

"Yes, I have been saying to my niece that we have been very fortunate to see such a performance. I realize that such things are said to be illusions, but there is no denying that the man performs wonders, not illusions." Mehitabel indicated one of the two unoccupied places at their table. "Missus Dovecote, it would be very kind of you if you would join us."

"Why certainly, Missus Reyns," Missus Dovecote said, taking one of the seats and smiling. "You were correct, I think, in saying that the Incredible Anton works wonders, but there are wonders all around us—think of the aeroplane."

"I've only seen one once. It was really frightening, to see that machine in the air. What will they think of next?" She signaled to the waiter. "Missus Dovecote will be sharing our table," she said, and then added, "We've only just had the soup. The Spanish soup with tomatoes and cucumbers is particularly nice. They serve it cold."

"That will be fine," Auralia Dovecote said. "The Spanish soup to start, and then I would like to see the menu." She looked at Mehitabel. "You strike me as a woman of great spiritual sensitivity. I am rarely wrong about such things."

"Oh!" exclaimed Mehitabel, flattered and confused. "I am very interested in spiritual matters, it's true, but I doubt I can call myself spiritually sensitive."

"You are too modest," Missus Dovecote insisted, completely ignoring Millicent. "So often this sensitivity comes with suffering, doesn't it?"

"Perhaps you're right," Mehitabel allowed as she finished the last of the tea in her cup and reached to pour more.

"I have been hoping," Missus Dovecote continued with great determination, "to have a sitting during the crossing."

"A sitting?" Mehitabel asked, staring in fascination at Auralia Dovecote.

"A séance. I have something of a gift as a psychic, and being on the water often enhances my powers." She looked up as the waiter brought her soup. "There are those who have told me that, this being the twentieth century, it is no longer fitting for us to have séances and other spiritual exercises, but I think that this is plainly false. When mankind has shown such progress and promise, what better time to seek for spiritual advancement as well?"

"Oh, yes!" Mehitabel said with feeling. "I agree with you completely, Missus Dovecote, and anything that I might do to be of assistance, you have only to ask me."

"I will bear that in mind. I feel that it would be best to begin soon, for with a voyage of this nature, it is important to know as much as possible." She gave a dark look to Mehitabel and began to eat her soup.

Mehitabel beamed, her eyes shining, as she looked at Millicent. "Isn't this wonderful? You will learn that the Incredible Anton isn't the only one who can produce marvels."

"He doesn't produce marvels," Millicent said, finding it hard to believe that even her aunt could be so credulous.

"Of course he does," said Mehitabel. "You saw what he did. You may call such things illusions, but it is apparent to me that he has skills and talents far beyond those of most men."

"I should say so," Missus Dovecote chimed in, between swallows. "It is not uncommon for those with great abilities to mask them so that others will accept them, and so that those who wish them ill may be deceived."

"But—" Millicent began, and stopped herself, recalling what Anton had told her about those who wished to be fooled. At the time she had doubted his wisdom, but she realized now that if these two women wanted to be taken in, it was not her place to argue with them. For one thing, they would probably not believe her, and for another, they would not thank her for her information.

"My niece is a great realist," Mehitabel said indulgently.

"She is always seeking out the reasons behind things. You would be astonished to learn of the way she pursues studies. Her father has said that she will have the makings of a scholar if she's not careful."

"I'm not certain that's becoming in a young woman," Missus Dovecote said with some severity. "This new effort to educate women is most often ill advised. There are too many women who seek to press beyond their natural limits, and you can see what it brings about."

Millicent wished that Miss Gordon were in the dining room and could hear this, for she knew that the stern young woman would have a great deal to say about such opinions. Her courage almost failed her, but she managed to say with an unfelt smile, "I think that it is wise to let females decide for themselves what their natural limits are." She felt her aunt give her a covert pinch on her arm, but went on as if it had not happened. "Some of us seek to broaden our minds."

"She's an enterprising child, isn't she?" Mehitabel asked Missus Dovecote archly. The two older women exchanged knowing glances.

"You have something yet to learn in manners," said Missus Dovecote in a lowered voice. "When you have mastered that, then you can turn your attention to your mind."

Before Millicent could protest, Mehitabel smoothed things over. "Time will tell which of us is right, and nothing we say right now can make much of a difference." She took a deep breath. "Now, about the sitting . . ."

By three that afternoon, it was decided. Missus Dovecote would come to Mehitabel and Millicent's cabin the next morning for a brief séance. Millicent was far too young to attend, both women said. It was agreed that they should invite two others to join them so that there would be sufficient numbers present to "contain the spirits," as Auralia Dovecote expressed it.

"I think it would be nice to invite Mister Geoffrey Wingham," Mehitabel said, almost blushing. "He is an attentive man, and very much a gentleman. He would not attempt to dissuade us in our venture."

"I believe that he will do," Missus Dovecote said after giving the name her consideration. "There are so few men to choose from. It would be most improper to invite the Incredible Anton, of course, for it would imply that we doubt his powers. The General, of course, is out of the question."

"What of Mister Dovecote?" Mehitabel ventured, regarding her new friend with interest.

"How I wish it were possible." Auralia Dovecote sighed. "His health makes it imprudent for him to have such experiences, and I fear that if we were to ask him to sit with us, it might have an adverse effect on him."

"How very trying for you," Mehitabel commiserated.

"Well, it is said that we are all tested in the fires of adversity," Missus Dovecote said with resignation. "I'm certain the purpose will be plain eventually."

"But whom else should we include?" Mehitabel asked, returning to the matter at hand.

"What about that poor Mister Homes?" Missus Dovecote suggested after another pause.

"Mister Homes. That sad little man?" Mehitabel asked, a bit taken aback. "Why do you think he might care to join us?"

"I'm not entirely sure," Missus Dovecote said. "There

is something about him, don't you think? There is an air of isolation that must yearn for something more."

"Oh," said Mehitabel, trying to understand what Missus Dovecote meant. "You clearly understand these matters better than I do. If you believe that he will help the sitting, I will extend the invitation."

"That would be best, I believe." Missus Dovecote, who had been occupying the deck chair next to Mehitabel, sat up, folding the blanket that had been over her knees. "I must prepare for this. I am grateful to you for permitting us to meet in your cabin, for I am convinced that it would be awkward to meet in ours. Mister Dovecote, you understand."

"Naturally," said Mehitabel. "I think that he must be blessed to have such a wife as you. There are many others who would not be amenable to aiding him as you do."

"As to that, we must deal with what fate sends us." She shook out the long tucks of her skirt. "Thank you again, Missus Reyns."

"Please call me Mehitabel," she said, knowing that she ought to be more reserved, but excusing herself because the ship gave her a sense of camaraderie that she ordinarily did not feel for strangers.

"And you must call me Auralia," said Missus Dovecote promptly. "It is odd to stand on ceremony in surroundings like these."

"My thought exactly," Mehitabel said, and watched her new friend make her way down the deck. She leaned back and smiled up at the sun. It was really very pleasant to be on this voyage, she thought, and decided that she must write a letter of appreciation to her brother, Haywood, at the first opportunity.

By evening, Mehitabel was determined to speak to Geoffrey Wingham as soon as he should appear in the Grand Salon. She was nervous now, for the idea of approaching a man, very probably an unmarried man, was so incorrect that she found it almost too distressing to think about.

"Is something the matter, Aunt Mehitabel?" Millicent asked as she watched her aunt fuss with her necklace.

"Not really," Mehitabel answered. "Nothing important."

"Is it about the séance you're planning with Missus Dovecote?" Millicent guessed shrewdly.

"Not directly, no, miss, and if it were, it is no concern of yours." She chose a second bracelet and clapped it onto her wrist.

"You know, I think one of the reasons they insist that first-class passengers dress for dinner every night," Millicent said while she adjusted her hair, "is to keep all of us from getting bored. The trouble is, changing clothes gets to be boring, as well."

"Persons of quality," said Mehitabel at her most quelling, "prefer to dress for dinner."

"Do they? Or are they just used to it?" Millicent asked, doing her best to appear innocent.

"That's quite enough, miss," Mehitabel said, and perfumed her wrists.

"Are you going to do it?" Millicent persisted.

"Do what?" Mehitabel asked in a vague tone of voice.

"Have a séance, of course. That's all you talked about earlier."

"Missus Dovecote is willing to try a sitting tomorrow morning at ten-thirty." It was all she wanted to say to her niece, knowing that Millicent was too curious for her own good.

"May I be there?" Millicent wanted to know. She leaned forward in her chair and waited for the answer.

"I think not. This isn't a game for children, you know." She raised her head and looked squarely at Millicent. "And that is all I am prepared to say to you, Millicent."

"Who else is coming?" Millicent asked, paying little attention to her aunt's warning.

"That is hardly your concern," Mehitabel reminded her. "You will not be here."

Millicent shrugged and went out with her aunt, determined to learn more of this séance.

By the end of the evening, Mehitabel had screwed up her courage and spoken to both gentlemen about the sitting, and both had accepted the invitation.

"So you see," she said to Auralia Dovecote as the two women said good night outside the Grand Salon, "we shall have their assistance in the morning."

"Excellent," Auralia said. "I am delighted to hear this, my dear. You are more than generous."

"It is you who are generous, Auralia," Mehitabel said as they reached the door.

Following behind them, Millicent had almost finished working out her plan.

In the morning, Mehitabel rang for the understeward and asked that a tray with tea and sweet rolls be brought in, explaining that she and a few of the other passengers would be passing the time together. "Make sure there is plenty of cream. It is always difficult to be sure there is adequate cream."

The understeward accepted her order and went off to

get what was required while Mehitabel busied herself in preparing the sitting room of their first-class suite for the sitting.

Auralia Dovecote arrived before the understeward returned. Her dress was of the first quality, of a mauve color with soft falls of lace at the cuffs. She wore a neat hat with a whisper veil and looked wonderfully ethereal. She greeted Mehitabel with affection and looked around the room.

"You've done very well," she said, consulting the watch that hung from a pin on her lapel. "The gentlemen should be here shortly."

"Yes, and so should the understeward," Mehitabel said. She herself had dressed with unusual care, having chosen a walking dress of light twill in a becoming shade of tea rose with deep lace insets at the throat and bosom. She had taken great pains with her hair and wore it in a modified version of the Gibson Girl style.

The understeward returned with a large tray with the requested tea, sweet rolls, and cream on it, and at Mehitabel's instruction placed it on the side table. He accepted Mehitabel's ten-cent gratuity with a nod and left the cabin.

"I do like the tea they serve on board, don't you?" Mehitabel asked her guest.

"It's very good, but for the prices they charge, everything ought to be of the best," Auralia said, not quite as spiritually as Mehitabel expected. "It is very important to get value for money."

"Yes, it certainly is," Mehitabel said, and went to open the door to the knock.

"Missus Reyns," said Geoffrey Wingham, coming into the cabin, "and Missus Dovecote; how good of you to include me in your séance. I have never attended one before, and I am honored by the opportunity you have given me."

Millicent, who had hidden in the closet in the bedroom of their cabin, now thought it was safe to come out, and she approached the connecting door so that she could observe what took place during the séance.

The four adults were seated around the low drumhead table, which had been cleared of all other material. They were all holding hands. Mister Homes, who had been the last to arrive, was fidgeting, clearly uneasy in this new situation. Missus Dovecote was starting to make a strange, moaning sound at the back of her throat, saying now and then, "We are calling on the spirits."

Mehitabel sat with her back to Millicent, but it was plain from her posture that she was more enthralled with what Missus Dovecote was doing than with what the Incredible Anton had done.

"This Big Wolf," Missus Dovecote declared in a deep voice that made Millicent have to stifle a giggle. "Him once heap big Indian brave."

"Oh!" Mehitabel breathed.

"She's most amazing," Mister Wingham said, going along with Mehitabel.

"No talk," Missus Dovecote ordered in her bass voice. "Not good talk while spirits present." There was a little silence while the sitters indicated they would be quiet.

"Why you call Big Wolf?"

"Um . . ." Mehitabel began, not certain that this was permission to speak or not. "We wish to learn wisdom, don't we?" She looked at the two men and saw Mister

Wingham nod in encouragement. "We want to hear what you have to tell us."

"Heap bad medicine on this canoe. Many deaths. Many come to spirits. Bad men here. Big Wolf no like."

Millicent listened, thinking that Missus Dovecote was overdoing it now. She found it hard to imagine her aunt could be so taken in by this act.

"Big Wolf give warning."

"Gracious," Mehitabel said faintly. "Of what?"

"There many here who not be what they claim. Many here." There was a brief pause, then the bass voice went on. "Big Wolf no stay here. Bad place. Bad man here." And with that final pronouncement, Missus Dovecote fell forward, facedown, onto the table.

6

"Auralia!" shrieked Mehitabel, releasing Mister Wingham's and Mister Homes's hands to reach out for the medium. "Are you all right? Speak up, please."

"My dear Missus Dovecote," Mister Wingham said at his most solicitous. "What has become of you?"

Mister Homes was silent, but Millicent could see that he was holding his hands clenched and that his knuckles were white. This puzzled her, for it seemed to Millicent that this was a peculiar reaction for so timid a man.

Missus Dovecote raised her head. "What happened?" she asked weakly.

"Oh, dear, don't you *know*?" Mehitabel gasped.

"I have no recollection of anything I say in trance," Missus Dovecote proclaimed, recovering rapidly and sitting up once more. "Who was it? Ling Lu or Big Wolf? Those are my two contacts on the Other Side."

"Big Wolf," said Mehitabel, very impressed with what

Missus Dovecote revealed. "He . . . he didn't stay long."

"He never does, thank goodness," Missus Dovecote said, her fingers tidying the drape of her skirts and fussing with lace at the neck of her dress. "He's always full of gloom. I gather that he hasn't found the Happy Hunting Ground."

"Who is Ling Lu?" Mehitabel could not help asking.

"My other guide. She's *much* nicer, and almost never has bad things to say. Where is the tea?"

Mehitabel got up at once and hastened to prepare a cup for Missus Dovecote. "How thoughtless of me," she said as she added cream and sugar.

"When I am finished with a sitting, however brief, I am always famished," Missus Dovecote told the room at large as she accepted the cup and saucer from Mehitabel. "So good of you to do this."

"I was quite impressed with the change in your voice," Mister Wingham said to Auralia Dovecote. "It was nothing like your own."

"Yes," said Missus Dovecote through a bit of sweet roll, "so I have been told. I understand that Ling Lu has an Oriental accent, as well."

"Mister Homes, you have been silent," Mehitabel said without criticizing him too sharply.

"I don't know what to say," the commonplace little man admitted. "I've never attended a séance before."

From her vantage point, Millicent could see that his hands were clenched once more. There was something about him that made him appear not shy but angry.

"It's always startling the first time, they tell me," Missus Dovecote remarked, adding, "It often puzzles me when I'm myself again, for I am aware that something has changed, but I never know what."

"And to think that this evening the Incredible Anton will be performing again," Mehitabel reminded them all. "This is a crossing filled with wonders."

"How fortunate for all of us," Mister Wingham seconded her.

Millicent decided to let herself out the side door and go for a walk on the deck, since nothing more of interest was likely to be learned now. She had completed her third time around the first-class deck when a voice spoke up from one of the chairs set out for the passengers.

"Have you finished your morning constitutional?" asked the Incredible Anton.

"It's not a constitutional," Millicent said. "I'm thinking."

"Is it anything you'd care to discuss?" he inquired, rising from the chair and walking along beside her.

"I don't know yet," she answered, having given the matter some thought.

"I am curious, naturally, but I don't intend to press you." He reached into his pocket and drew out a long, dark cheroot. "Do you mind if I smoke?"

"Go ahead," she told him, her thoughts still on the séance. "Have you ever seen spirits?"

"You mean ghosts and the like?" Anton asked with some surprise as he struck a match.

"I guess so," Millicent said. "Or mediums in a trance? Have you seen anything like that? Do you know how it's done?"

He finished lighting his cigar before answering. "I've never seen a medium, no, at least not a legitimate one. I've seen any number of shams, some of them very convincing, with trumpets and tambourines whizzing around the room. I've seen several versions of the Spirit Box—in fact, I do that one myself, when I have a larger theater to work in. Why?"

"Nothing," she replied, knowing that her manners were very bad.

"I take it your aunt is interested in spiritualism," Anton guessed. "Women of her age and background usually are. They're also the ones who think what I do is miraculous."

"Missus Dovecote has a spirit guide named Big Wolf, and another one called Ling Lu." Millicent spoke in a rush, fearing that she should not speak of this at all.

"Big Wolf and Ling Lu. Not very original. For some reason, most trance mediums these days have Red Indians and Orientals for guides. Fifty years ago, it was ancient Egyptians and medieval wizards." He drew on his cheroot and exhaled slowly. "I take it there's been a séance?"

"Yes," Millicent admitted, troubled now at what she revealed.

"Don't worry, I won't give you away. I gather you weren't invited." He did not need to hear her answer. "What did Big Wolf have to say? If you'd rather not tell me, it's all right."

Millicent considered saying nothing, but what she had heard disturbed her enough to make her tell him. "He said that bad things and bad people were aboard, and that many weren't what they appeared, or something like that."

"Not very original. In any group, there are bound to be a few undesirables. And as to the rest, you will learn that very few of us are what we seem." The Incredible Anton looked out to sea, a remote expression on his aristocratic face.

"Including you?" asked Millicent, unable to resist the question.

"Certainly. Perhaps someday I'll tell you about it." He strolled on beside her, neither of them speaking, enjoying their companionable silence. Finally he said, "You'll be at the performance tonight."

"I plan to be," she replied.

"Good. Tomorrow you can tell me what your aunt thinks of my illusions. If she is captivated by spirits named Big Wolf, she'll doubtless be overcome by my 'Princess and the Flame.' It's my own, and I'm rather proud of it." He smiled at her. "And you can tell me how you think it's done."

"All right," said Millicent, accepting the challenge with alacrity. "I'll watch very carefully."

Anton chuckled. "Those who think they watch carefully are often the most easily fooled. Keep that in mind, and that's all the advice I'm going to give you." He continued along beside her for another circuit of the deck, then excused himself. "I haven't finished setting up for our performance, and my assistant, Sabina, hasn't worked on this makeshift stage yet."

"I'll help, if you like," Millicent offered.

At this, Anton laughed outright. "That would give you too much of an advantage, Millicent. Another time, I might permit it." He waved once as he walked away, stopping only to put out his cigar before going indoors.

That evening, there was a great deal of excitement among the first-class passengers, for after the taste they had had of the art of the Incredible Anton, they were eager to see what he could produce for them with a fully mounted show.

Captain Symington spoke for the entire gathering when he came to the front of the stage in the Grand Ballroom and said, "We've all heard the comment 'Here is a man who needs no introduction,' which is most often followed by a long harangue. I'm not going to subject you to that, because after his previous demonstration, the Incredible Anton truly needs none. Ladies and gentlemen, please welcome him."

As soon as the Captain left the stage, the velvet curtains parted and the Incredible Anton came out to accept his applause. As he bowed, he reached out and plucked a gold coin from the air. He held it up, examined it, reached out, and pulled another one out of the air. At that, he signaled for his assistant, and a very attractive young woman in a very attractive and scandalously low-backed dress came out, carrying a bucket, which Anton made a show of turning upside down to make it clear it was empty before dropping the two coins into it, letting them ring before finding the next coin, and the next, and the next. In all, he dropped forty-two coins into the bucket before turning to the audience and bowing.

When the applause died down, he said, "I find that money often gets the attention of most persons." He let the polite laughter ripple as he tugged his sleeves up to his elbows, unfastened his cuff links, and rolled up his shirt cuffs as well. "Most persons suppose," he explained, "that magicians hide things up their sleeves, so I am doing my best to show that this is not how I perform this next effect." He signaled and the curtain was lowered, leaving him alone on the narrow apron. "While my assistants are setting up the stage, I'd like to tell you a brief story about this next illusion. It seems that the immortal Robert Houdin, the famous French conjuror of the last century, was sent to Africa to quell an uprising. General Cuernos, I wonder if you might be willing to help me with this?"

The General looked affronted and started to refuse. "I am not party to such—"

"This always works better with a military man," Anton went on smoothly, as if there had been no objection. "For one thing, I am certain of a military man's aim, and in this illusion, that is most important."

"Aim?" the General asked, not wanting to show that he was confused. "Why should my aim matter to a magician?"

"Because I want you to fire a rifle at me," Anton said at his most urbane. "So that I can catch the bullet in my teeth."

"Madness," General Cuernos scoffed.

"Humor me, then," Anton said, a charming smile on his face. He signaled, and Jibben came onto the stage with a Winchester rifle in his hands. Anton took it and held it up. "General, if you would?"

Muttering, General Cuernos made his way to the front of the stage and stood glaring up at Anton. "What is it?"

"I would like you to examine this rifle and assure the audience that it is genuine and in good working order." He handed the weapon to the General and stepped back. "Take your time." The curtains were drawn open, and it was with some apprehension that the audience saw an enormous bull's-eye set in place on the stage.

"It is genuine and appears to be in good order," the General admitted grudgingly.

"Then will you examine this bullet?" He came forward,

took the rifle, and handed the bullet to the General while he opened the breech of the rifle.

"It is a bullet," the General agreed, and handed it back to Anton, who gave both the Winchester and the bullet to the General.

"Load it for me, will you, please?"

"I will," the General said, running out of patience with the whole thing. "There."

"Very good, and thank you. Now, if you will do one last thing and walk to the rear of the audience, take aim at my mouth, and fire?" As he gave these instructions, he went and stood so that his head was at the center of the bull's-eye. "Fire whenever you are ready, General."

General Cuernos stomped back to the last row of chairs and stood for a moment before lifting the rifle, taking careful aim.

The sound in that enclosed room was enormous. Everyone in the audience jumped, and three of the women screamed.

The Incredible Anton stepped forward, his mouth partly open, something small lodged between his teeth. He reached up and removed it. "General, one last favor, if you will?"

General Cuernos was staring at Anton with an expression of disbelief mingled with disgust. "What now?"

"Will you examine this and identify it as a bullet like the one fired from that rifle?" He gestured his encouragement while there were whispers and exclamations from the audience.

"So long as you do not expect me to accept this as any sort of miracle. There has to be a trick to it!" the General growled as he came forward, still holding the rifle.

"There is naturally a trick to it," Anton said without any loss of composure. "If there were not, I would be a corpse lying on the stage at this very moment."

"How can he do such things?" Mehitabel whispered to Millicent. "How can there be a trick to anything so dangerous?"

"That's probably why he needs the trick," Millicent said softly.

General Cuernos took the bullet and looked at it. "This is the same caliber and variety of bullet that you gave me to load, certainly, but I will not say that it is the same one." He gave the Incredible Anton a defiant stare, handed him the rifle, and returned to his seat, his whole manner rigid with disapproval.

"Ladies and gentlemen, please give the General your applause for all his assistance," said Anton as Jibben appeared to claim the rifle. "For the final illusion this evening, we will perform an illusion of my own invention—the 'Princess and the Flame.' " As he spoke, the bull's-eye was moved aside to reveal Sabina seated on a high swing. She was dressed in lavish and opulent robes, with a diamond tiara set in her brunette hair. Light flashed from the jewels at her throat and ears and shone from the gold-and-silver-spangled lace that trimmed the bosom of her gown.

The audience made an appreciative flurry of applause.

"You're very gracious," said Anton, as he approached the swing, rolling down his sleeves once more as he did. "Princess, are you ready?"

"I am," answered Sabina in a low, pleasant voice.

Anton took a long, heavy cord that dangled from one side of the swing and began to walk around her, pulling the two supporting ropes into an ever-tightening twisted strand. When the swing and its splendid rider had been wound to the limit, and raised more than five feet off the stage, Anton, holding the cord, said to the audience, "When this is released, as you are all aware, the tension on the ropes will be freed and the swing will spin. But watch closely, ladies and gentlemen, if you please, for this is no ordinary swing, and there is more being changed here than the direction the swing moves." With this announcement, he gave a snap with the cord; it fell away and the swing began to turn.

The audience stared as the spin grew faster, and the gorgeous robes of the Princess fanned out around the swing, flashing colors until she and the costume became a beautiful, mesmerizing blur.

"Now!" the Incredible Anton shouted.

There was a puff of bright smoke and a muffled explosion, and where the Princess had hung before, there was now a St. Catherine's Wheel, turning and shooting out its many-colored flames.

There was a long intake of breath, and then the audience burst into applause.

Anton clapped his hands once: the St. Catherine's Wheel vanished, and the Incredible Anton bowed deeply. "Thank you, ladies and gentlemen. In our next performance, we will perform the very dangerous Iron Maiden for you."

"It's not possible," Mehitabel said to Millicent. "He's not going to convince me that it's all tricks. That man is truly a magician. How else could he do that?"

"I'm not sure," Millicent said slowly, and added to herself, "yet."

7

The large room where Anton's show was stored carried steerage passengers when the *Duchess of Malfi* was bound for New York; now it was empty, as were most of the other barrackslike accommodations for the impoverished immigrants. Only one of the six steerage rooms had any occupants, and that was the smallest, carrying fifteen members of the same Portuguese family back to Lisbon for the ceremony that would make one of their older cousins a cardinal of the Roman Catholic Church.

"Better check the wheel on the back of the Iron Maiden," Anton was saying to Jibben when Millicent found them the following morning. "Make sure it moves smoothly."

Sabina, dressed now in sensible and fashionable linen with a taffeta coat over her high-waisted morning gown, came up to Anton, saying with a decidedly lower-class English accent, "I lost some spangles last night. And I don't like that box, Duke. I don't like how close the spikes come when I'm in it."

Anton shook his head and smiled at her without much warmth. "It might be a good idea to stay away from cream puffs for a while, then. You'll fit this and the other cabinets better if you do."

"Are you calling me fat?" Sabina demanded harshly.

"No, but I am saying that these cabinets were made for you while you were slimmer and it wouldn't be a bad idea to keep that in mind." He was about to walk away, but Sabina was not quite finished.

"How am I supposed to find a husband if I stay a scrawny, bone-chested girl, tell me that."

"A year ago you didn't worry about finding husbands," Anton reminded her patiently. "Why now?"

"That was then. I'm over twenty now, and it's time I looked to my future before I have to settle for whoever will have me." She put one hand on her hip. "It's all very well for you, up with the nobs in first class, bowing and scraping away; I have to look among the johnnies in second class, and I mean to make the most of my chance. I can't be your assistant forever, and I'd rather die than go back to where I came from. You don't know what it was like, living the way I did when I was growing up. Whitechapel wouldn't be a decent place for diseased pigs to live."

"You're right, Sabina, I wouldn't know about that. I was too busy watching a mob massacre my father and uncle and three brothers instead." He stopped, seeing Millicent in the doorway. "I'm not going to compare misfortunes with you, Sabina. Each of us has some inner pain to endure. If you're worried about the Iron Maiden, you have only to be a bit thinner or to wear tighter corsets. It's your choice which you do." He left his assistant standing by the table with what looked like a very sophisticated doll in Turkish costume sitting on it.

"You said I could come and speak with you this morning," Millicent said, aware that she had overheard things that she was not intended to know.

"So I did, and you're most welcome here. You'll have to forgive Sabina her outbursts; she is always concerned about the Iron Maiden. It's one of the few times she is in any real danger during a performance, and it bothers her." He was smoothly polite as always, but there was something at the back of his eyes that made Millicent think that he was making more of an effort than usual to appear that way.

"It would bother me, as well," Millicent said. "Just as the bullet bothered me, though I think I might have figured out one way to do it."

"Have you?" Anton's smile grew more convincing. "Very well, tell me what you've deduced."

Millicent relaxed. "Well, first, whatever else was done, the bullet the gun fires can't be real."

"That's sensible. Go on." He glanced at Sabina as she left the room in a huff, bound for the second-class deck for a stroll.

"So if you gave the General a real bullet to look at, you had the means to substitute a false one." She looked up, hoping that he would encourage her.

"Your logic is very good, but do you have a method for doing this?" He waited, his face appreciative.

"Not yet, but I will." She did not like having to admit

this, but she knew better than to pretend to have knowledge. "I think I have a better notion about the 'Princess and the Flame,' " she went on.

"All right," he said. "Just a moment and we'll go out for a walk around the deck. Jibben, tend to that mechanism, will you?"

Jibben made an affirmative gesture and went back to his tasks.

"Your assistant is English?" Millicent asked as they went up the nearest companionway.

"They're both English. Jibben is an English Gypsy. Sabina is a Londoner. I had twenty-three people working in the show in New York, but the others preferred to stay in America, and so I will have to hire and train more assistants when I reach Europe." He held the door for her so that they could go out onto the deck. "There are several illusions we can't perform because we haven't enough people for them."

"I wondered about that," Millicent admitted. It was a brisk day, and she was glad of her light coat. She carried her hat in her hand and hoped that she would not encounter her aunt, who would insist she put it on.

"There are other illusions we can't perform for other reasons, such as the movement of the ship, but most of them require more than two assistants. I don't think I could borrow one of the understewards and train him overnight, do you?" He smiled again, enjoying their conversation.

"But the things you're doing all can be done with two assistants and on a ship," Millicent said, to make sure she had understood correctly.

"That's right. Also, remember that the stage is small

and does not have deep wings or a real fly gallery, to say nothing of the problems with lighting. Still, I think we're doing fairly well." He waited, then said, "About the 'Princess and the Flame'?"

"Oh," Millicent began, uncertain now that she had her opportunity that she had got it right. "It's only a guess, mind."

"Of course," Anton agreed.

"Well, that costume has a lot to do with it, not just because it's all shiny, but because it fans out and flashes the way it does. When it really spins, it holds the eyes."

"Very good," Anton approved. "Yes, you're right about holding the eyes. It also puts the audience into a very accepting state of mind, the way some persons do with a swinging pendulum or a spiral disk. Once you have caught the eyes that way, they are half convinced already." He gave her a gesture indicating that she should go on.

"Well, I noticed that there was a lot of costume and much of it was stiff, even when it was spinning. I think that your assistant got out of it before the puff of smoke." This was the thing she was least certain of, and she spoke with less confidence.

"*Very* good, Millicent. Some of my colleagues miss that point." He nodded, satisfied. "Do you know when this happens?"

"Well, at one point you crossed the stage in front of her. I didn't actually see anything, but that was probably it." Her anxiety almost made her hold her breath waiting for his response.

"You're right," he said, adding, "Always remember that nothing that happens during a magic show happens by chance. Everything is part of the illusion, no matter how minor or unconnected it may appear to be." He ticked off her points on his fingers. "So, you have established that the costume is part of the effect, that the spinning is a certain kind of distraction, and that Sabina leaves the stage before the costume does. What else?"

"The puff of smoke lets you get rid of the costume?" she suggested. "And the St. Catherine's Wheel is raised up from the floor during the confusion." She was more confident of these ideas and said them quickly.

"Brava!" Anton applauded. "You're thinking very clearly, and you're much more observant than most of the audience. I'm impressed, Millicent."

She blushed, because she recognized the sincerity in his voice. She decided to take a chance and ask him something that had been on her mind since they met. "Would you tell me what kind of accent you have? Your English is wonderful, but every now and then I notice that you shift emphasis or do something else that makes me think that you spoke another language before English."

"I speak eight languages." He paused, then, making up his mind, he went on, "But you're right, English is not my first language. I was born in Bohemia."

"Bohemia!" she exclaimed. "That's part of Austro-Hungary, isn't it? Prague is the old Bohemian capital, isn't it?" She was trying to remember her geography lessons, not at all certain that she had it right.

"You're mostly correct," he said quietly. "Praha," he went on, giving the city its Czech pronunciation, "is still considered the center of Bohemia by some."

She sensed that he did not like talking about his background, and so she changed the subject. "I was born in Pennsylvania; Mother and Father were there for a meeting about business and Father had insisted that she come with him. She still gets angry about it, sometimes." Satisfied that he was no longer on guard, she resumed discussing his performance. "The coins out of the air. I wonder if you do have them up your sleeve?"

"That would be one place," he said.

"They could be somewhere else on you, in the lining of your coat in some way." She shook her head. "But how you could walk without the coins clinking, I don't know."

"Quite a puzzle, isn't it?" He continued to walk with her, keeping silent while she thought.

"They aren't in the bucket already, you made that clear. I think you did, anyway."

"You're a very astute young lady," he said, but would not elaborate. "When you've worked it out, tell me what you have decided. You've done excellently so far, if that encourages you."

"Thank you." She wanted to ask him what he had meant about his father and uncle and brothers, but that would have meant admitting that she had overheard, which might anger the Incredible Anton. "I'll watch closely for your next performance."

"I'm not surprised," he said with a chuckle. "I'll be waiting to hear what you have to say."

"Good." They continued their walk in silence, both content in each other's company. Millicent was aware that her tall companion had adapted his pace to hers, so that she would not have to trot along at his side to keep up. She liked him for that, since so few adults were willing to do it, or if they did, they made a point of mentioning it. To his credit, Anton did neither of these things; he merely ambled as if it were the most natural thing in the world.

"Has your aunt attended any more séances?" Anton asked after a while.

"She would like another sitting, or so she told me. She thinks that Missus Dovecote is a great spiritualist. She thinks that you can really catch bullets in your teeth, too."

Anton laughed aloud. "I hope I never have to end up on the rough side of your tongue, Millicent."

"Only foolish people make me talk this way," she responded, feeling oddly embarrassed but pleased that he did not praise her for being clever or cute. That was what her father always did, and she hated it.

"There are a great many fools in the world, Millicent," he said, gently and seriously. "The best of them know they're fools. As you will probably learn to your sorrow."

"What do you mean?" Millicent said with genuine curiosity.

"Most fools think they are wise. I would rather deal with your aunt's honest credulity than with General Cuernos, for example; he is the greater fool of the two of them, you realize." He paused. "You see, your aunt has few pretenses, and knows what they are. The General long ago assumed that his pretenses were his dignity and his honor."

Millicent nodded. "And Aunt Mehitabel wouldn't make that mistake? She's always convinced that the right hat or the proper length of gloves will tell you all you need to know about a person. That's her dignity." She waited for him to go on, thinking with a shock that she was actually having a philosophical discussion for the first time in her life.

"Those are little vanities. No one will have to die or be turned out of her house if they have the wrong gloves; she will merely be impolite to them. The General, on the other hand, has it within his power to set an army marching if he is offended." He stopped walking. "How did I get onto these matters?"

"We were talking about fools," Millicent said sadly, knowing that their philosophical discussion was over.

"So we were," Anton agreed. "And we are the fools, walking around the deck when they are serving lunch in the dining room. Would you care to join me, or do you think your aunt would not approve?"

"I will be delighted to join you," said Millicent. "My aunt will probably be sitting with Missus Dovecote and be glad that she has the chance to converse without interruption." While she was not certain this was the case, she knew it was an argument that would persuade Aunt Mehitabel that she was trying to consider her feelings as well as taking care of her own entertainment.

"I'm not sure I believe you, but let that pass," said Anton. "I'm hungry, and it's refreshing to have someone intelligent to dine with. Most of those who ask to share my table want me to do card tricks all through the meal, or they are seeking the chance to learn how I do an effect, or want to challenge me on what they have seen. You're not planning to do any of those things, are you?"

"I don't think so," Millicent answered seriously.

"Then come on," he said, lengthening his stride a bit, but not so much that she had to run.

8

There was a third member of the party at Mehitabel's table; Mister Geoffrey Wingham sat with Missus Dovecote and Mehitabel, all three apparently engrossed in conversation. It was noticeable that Mister Wingham was being most attentive to Mehitabel.

"What do you think?" asked Anton, indicating Mister Wingham.

Millicent shrugged. "Aunt Mehitabel likes him, I think, but I don't know why."

Anton shook his head. "Oh yes you do. He's a man who knows how to make himself charming, and unless I miss my guess, your aunt has had precious little of that in her life." He looked over the menu as he spoke. "There's a broiled chicken in mustard sauce. How does that sound to you?"

Mehitabel laughed at something Mister Wingham had

said, and Missus Dovecote wagged a finger at him in joking reproof.

"I think I'd like the crabs' legs in cheese sauce instead. Once I get to school, I won't get a chance to have crabs' legs. There's always plenty of chicken." She cocked her head to the side. "Why did you say that about Aunt Mehitabel?"

"Oh, the way she looks, always anxious, eager to please, and complimented by trifles. That means she is not used to kindness. She's a widow, isn't she?"

Millicent nodded. "Her husband died a few years ago. My father's been looking after her ever since."

"That's not a very happy life," Anton said seriously.

"I suppose not," Millicent said, not completely sure what Anton was getting at.

"Mister Wingham came to the sitting, didn't he?" asked Anton.

"Yes; so did Mister Homes. Mister Wingham seemed to like it, but I don't think Mister Homes did," Millicent said, reading what was listed for dessert.

"Mister Homes is a bit of an enigma," Anton said, almost to himself.

"He's strange," Millicent agreed. "He acts like he's scared, but . . ." She faltered, not knowing how to describe what she had observed.

Anton met her eyes. "Precisely," he said with emphasis.

"Do you think the séances are done the same way as your illusions?" Millicent asked.

"Some of them are; I told you about that. Missus Dovecote isn't that type, I don't think, though she'd probably love to attend such a séance. There are times the most serious are the most gullible."

Millicent reflected on what Anton said. "I think she wants to believe in Ling Lu and Big Wolf, don't you?"

"Probably," he answered. "Mind you, Millicent, there are some who are studying the world beyond our senses who achieve some remarkable things, but not the sort of thing Missus Dovecote does."

Then the waiter was at their table and their most pressing talk was about food.

"We're going to have another séance," Mehitabel announced to Millicent that afternoon while Millicent was reading in their cabin.

"Oh?" Millicent said, looking up from her copy of *Pamela* by Richardson.

"Tomorrow afternoon. Auralia has said that she is willing to try again. Isn't she brave?" Mehitabel had just changed into an afternoon walking dress of puce and was adjusting her cartwheel hat with three curled ostrich plumes.

"I suppose so," Millicent said. "Why are you doing it?"

"Well," Mehitabel said with an air of mystery, "there are so many questions that Big Wolf created in our minds. Mister Wingham said that he was caught by the sense of foreboding that filled the room when the manifestation occurred."

"I see," Millicent said, trying to sound interested.

"When you're young, you don't know how life can leave a mark on you," Mehitabel said with a trace of petulance. "When you're older, you'll know what I mean. It's so hard to appreciate the joys of youth while you have them."

Millicent had heard this before from most of her adult relatives and was truly fed up with being told she did not appreciate her own youth. It was her private opinion that most of her older relatives had forgotten some of the difficulties of being young while enlarging on the advantages. She made herself smile and say, "I try to, Aunt Mehitabel."

"I hope so," Mehitabel said dubiously. "What I intended to tell you, however, is that since we are having this séance, I would like to arrange for you to do your reading in the lounge tomorrow. I'm certain that I can arrange it with Captain Symington this evening. Would that suit you, do you think?"

"I think it will," Millicent said, fully determined to watch the second session as well. "If not, I can probably watch the Incredible Anton rehearse."

Mehitabel gave her a searching look. "You've been quite cozy with that magician," she said, making the observation sound more like an accusation.

"He's interesting. He lets me guess about how he does the illusions."

"So long as that's all he does. Those people in the theater, you know, are not to be trusted. If he does anything that isn't right, you're to tell me about it at once." Mehitabel folded her arms. "At once, do you understand me?"

"Yes, Aunt Mehitabel." She had had warnings of this sort before, but it was only in the last year that she had come to learn what it was that "not right" meant. It offended Millicent that her aunt would suspect Anton of such behavior, or that she would tolerate it.

"That's a good girl. On a ship like this, I'm certain even a theatrical person is going to be circumspect, but it's wise to be cautious, in any event." She went to the door, opening it before adding, "It should please you to know that Mister Wingham will sit with us at dinner tonight."

"All right," Millicent said, not caring one way or the other.

"I know that it's not easy to be friendly with new acquaintances, but it would be good of you to make the effort." She closed the door, leaving Millicent to go back to reading Richardson.

The following afternoon Millicent waited until all four of the séance sitters were in place before she let herself in the side door and took up her position in the darkened bedroom.

"I feel the presence of the spirits," intoned Missus Dovecote, sounding as if she were half asleep.

"Can you call upon them, Auralia?" Mehitabel asked, eager to continue the adventure.

"I pray I have the strength." Missus Dovecote sighed, and then started to moan. "I call upon the spirits. I call upon the spirits." Her voice became fainter and fainter, turning into a thin, high wail.

Millicent came as close to the door as she dared and peered through the crack into the sitting room. She saw Missus Dovecote slumped in her chair, her head thrown back and her mouth half open.

"Oh, Auralia," whispered Mehitabel.

Then, as before, there was a sudden change and Missus Dovecote sat up at attention and spoke in that same bass voice. "Why you call Big Wolf again?"

"We . . . we have some questions," Mehitabel said in an uncertain tone.

"What questions? Why you ask questions?" Big Wolf sounded annoyed. "Not want talk now."

"You must," Mehitabel said, sounding more frightened than before. "We must have answers."

"Big Wolf not want questions." Missus Dovecote rolled her head from side to side. "Bad place. Many bad things."

"What bad things?" Mister Wingham demanded.

"Bad men. Not believe spirits." Missus Dovecote threw back her head and howled. "Bad storm come. Bad seas. Big Wolf see dead men, many more come to spirit world."

"But why? How?" Mehitabel asked, more distressed than the two men.

"Battle. Big battle," Big Wolf growled. "Bad men want rule world. Bad men do bad things to others. Big Wolf not want to stay here with bad men."

"Is there anyone on this ship who is a bad man?" Mehitabel asked, trying to stay calm.

"Bad men. Not want spirits here." There was a garbled word or two, and then Big Wolf went on. "Heap big danger. Many dangers. Big Wolf see much trouble. In spirit world there are many worries."

"What does that mean?" Mister Wingham asked, honestly confused.

"Spirit world see trouble. Spirit world have all knowledge. Big Wolf tell men that much bad coming. Bad weather. Bad ship. Bad men. Big Wolf no like it here." Missus Dovecote gave a shudder, her head shook, and then she said in a high, lisping voice, "This be spirit Ling Lu. What honorable persons want of spirits?"

"Is this the Oriental Princess?" asked Mehitabel in an awed voice.

"So sorry to correct honorable querents, but in spirit world there is no rank. Ling Lu was princess while in the world. Here she is only Ling Lu." Missus Dovecote was sitting differently, her posture more deferential than when Big Wolf was speaking.

"Big Wolf said that there are bad men on this ship," said Mehitabel. "What did he mean? Can you tell us?"

"Ling Lu not know what Big Wolf mean. Ling Lu does not wish to argue with Big Wolf. It is wrong for spirits to disagree. Ling Lu will not disagree with Big Wolf."

"But does that mean that there are bad men or that there aren't?" asked Geoffrey Wingham, less patient than Mehitabel.

"In your world, there are many bad men. That is the fate of your life. Ling Lu not want to trouble those attending sitting, but is true that some passengers are hiding facts." Missus Dovecote sighed loudly. "In spirit world, we have much sympathy for the honorable querents. Not easy to learn which persons are worthy and which are not. Ling Lu cannot advise."

"Then why did you come?" asked Mehitabel, disappointment showing in the way she sat.

"Spirits summoned. Ling Lu obey." There was another pause and then the soft, sibilant words went on, "Ling Lu not want to worry honorable querents. Ling Lu sorry that there is confusion. Ling Lu want all honorable querents to learn tranquillity. Nothing is wrong that cannot be fixed."

"Then something is wrong?" Mister Wingham inquired.

"Always something wrong in world of flesh. Ling Lu sorry to tell honorable querents this, but it is great truth. Ling Lu say that all wrongs are righted in time. Ling Lu sees honorable querents in worry and other feelings. Ling

Lu not wish them to be so. If world of flesh is bad, world of spirit can help. If there is death and war, it is only in world of flesh."

"Are you saying that there will be death and war?" Mister Wingham asked sharply.

"There is always death. There is always war. They come in world of flesh, and world of flesh is part of that. World of spirit not have war and death. This is the way things are." Missus Dovecote moaned and shuddered, her whole body trembling.

"Auralia! Are you all right?" Mehitabel asked in alarm.

"Medium is tiring," said the voice of Ling Lu. "Fatigue is part of world of flesh, too. Honorable querents should not ask Ling Lu to remain much longer. If honorable querents summon spirits again, do not tire medium as much. Not good for medium to be tired. Medium not know how to end trance when so tired."

"Oh, the poor woman." Mehitabel sighed.

"Ling Lu have no wish to cause more trouble, but Ling Lu ought to say that ship has impostors aboard. Many men are impostors in world of flesh. It is wise to think of these things. Impostors are not good men, but not always bad men, either."

"That's very helpful," Mister Wingham said sarcastically. "I wonder if the Princess would tell us a little more?"

Millicent leaned closer to the door and waited to hear what the comment might be. She saw that the only person who was not engrossed in what Missus Dovecote was saying in that strange, lisping voice was Mister Homes, who sat absolutely still, his rodent face as still as if he might be trying to hide.

"Ling Lu must go now, before medium is harmed by

trance. All honorable querents are much in her debt for this." The soft voice began to disappear entirely, the last two words being almost inaudible. Missus Dovecote gave an eerie cry and slumped in her chair.

Mehitabel leaned forward at once and began to chafe the medium's wrists. "Do you think I ought to unfasten her collar, Mister Wingham?"

Geoffrey Wingham shook his head. "She is not of high color, and her breathing is regular. It may be that she does not need this service at all. Give her a little time, and if there is no appearance of recovery, I myself will go for the ship's doctor to tend her." He gave Mehitabel a concerned look. "And you, Missus Reyns, how are you faring? You seem a little overset."

"I thank you for your asking," said Mehitabel, looking up from fussing over Auralia Dovecote. "It is nothing to bother about, and Auralia has far greater need than I do. I hope she wakens soon."

As if responding to a cue, Missus Dovecote raised her head. "Dear me. How long was I senseless this time?"

Mehitabel was astonished at how calm her friend was, and she remarked, "How can you be so tranquil, my dear, after what has transpired? I am all over fidgets."

"Well"—Missus Dovecote laughed as she sat up in her chair—"since I don't *know* what transpired, it is not difficult to be quite at ease about it." She reached up to fuss with her elaborate hairstyle. "I learned long since to be cautious with these occurrences. The first time I had a formal sitting, I was actually foolish enough to leave my hat on, but now I have learned that the most sensible thing to do is to be prepared for a sudden loss of consciousness that the spirits visit upon me." She fiddled with the cuffs of her dress and then stood up. "I'm famished. This always happens when the spirits have been busy. Who was it this time?" She looked at Mehitabel for an answer.

"Both of them," Mehitabel said, obviously impressed with this announcement.

"Both! Goodness, no wonder I feel as light-headed as I do." She laughed a bit uncertainly. "I want to change for dinner, but before I leave, will you be kind enough to see if we might have some sandwiches or a tea brought up? I'm sure I'll be unable to wait for dinner."

"How can you be so prosaic about this?" asked Mehitabel in amazement. "You have just spent more than half an hour with the spirits."

"More to the point, you have spent the time with them. I have been the medium, and that's all." She looked at Mister Wingham and then Mister Homes. "Will either or both of you gentlemen be kind enough to procure tea for us?"

Both of them responded at once, Mister Wingham saying, "It would be an honor, Missus Dovecote," and Mister Homes simply executing a crisp, almost Prussian bow.

"He is a strange little man," Missus Dovecote said when the two men had left the room.

"Mister Wingham?" asked Mehitabel, astonished at the comment.

"Gracious, no. Mister Homes. Mister Wingham is very much the gentleman, and very pleasing in his manners, if a little casual. I assume it is the setting." She chose the small sofa and sank down upon it. "You'll have to tell me what Ling Lu and Big Wolf said. I'm always worried that they might become improper."

"They might," Mehitabel agreed, coloring a bit, "but they did not on this occasion."

Millicent wondered what the women meant by improper. She most often heard the term in relation to behavior, and from what she had seen, behavior did not apply to spirits, if there were such things. She wished she could ask Missus Dovecote about it, but knew that she dared not.

"Men do not understand these things," Missus Dovecote declared, adding quietly, "and I'm sure I prefer it the way it is."

"In these matters, you are undoubtedly correct," Mehitabel answered, leaving Millicent pondering what they meant.

9

The shuffleboard courts painted on the deck were deserted but for Millicent, who was competing against herself. It was here that Mehitabel found her almost an hour later.

"It's time you were changing for dinner, child," she said as she watched Millicent send yet another puck sliding toward the others.

"There's enough time for me to finish the game," Millicent said, not paying much attention.

"I'm sorry you could not be included in the sitting this afternoon, but there are matters that are best left to adults," Mehitabel said, convinced that Millicent was feeling neglected.

"That's all right. I hope it went well?" She was curious to see how much her aunt would reveal.

"It was very stimulating. Missus Dovecote is a very gifted medium and her spirit guides are fascinating."

"Good." Her red pucks were ahead of her blue ones;

Millicent decided that she would have to work harder for blue.

"I don't want you to be upset when we exclude you," Mehitabel persisted.

"I'm not upset," Millicent assured her, taking care not to add that she was not truly excluded, either.

One of the understewards walked by in the company of the first officer. He said to the officer, "We cannot find him at all. He is not in the crews' quarters, and the others haven't seen him since last night. You realize that with this second understeward missing, the crew are concerned."

"What about the doctor? Have you talked to . . ." The rest was lost as the two men passed out of earshot.

Millicent looked after them. "Do you think someone else is missing?"

Mehitabel shuddered. "I hope not. But these understewards, you know, are not always trustworthy."

"But where would such a man go?" Millicent asked reasonably. "There's only so much room on a ship, even a big liner like this one." She sent her last puck slithering down the deck and grinned as red won.

"They'll find him," Mehitabel predicted. "Probably the worse for drink. I recall that Haywood had a housekeeper when he first bought the summer place in Newport, and that woman never drank less than a pint of gin a day. Servants cannot be trusted, Millicent. It's sad, but it is also true."

Millicent was willing to give up her shuffleboard now that she was finished with her game. "They probably think the same things of their employers," she said in her most steady tone.

"You're not serious, are you?" Mehitabel asked with feeling. "It is not fitting for those of us in our level of society to abuse those in our care." She paused. "I suppose, where maids are concerned, matters are sadly different. It is unfortunate that most maids have lax morals, or that their masters are so willing to take advantage of their naïveté."

"Perhaps the maids are not as willing as the masters like to think," Millicent said. "Mister Armbrewster said that his wife's maid enticed him, but the judge still insisted that it was rape." Millicent saw the shock in Mehitabel's face and knew that she had gone too far.

"Young lady, don't you *ever* let your father know you have any knowledge of such scandal! It isn't fitting for you to read about such matters, or to discuss them. Ladies do not sully themselves with such sordid gossip." She indicated the door to the corridor. "And I don't want to hear you speaking of anything of this nature again."

"All right," Millicent said, disappointed but not surprised by this order.

"And if you ever hear anyone talking about these unsavory matters, I want you to be sure you let them know that it is wrong to perpetuate gossip." She looked as haughty as she knew how to, which was not very. "You mustn't let yourself be dragged down to their level. Persons who do not have any breeding can be a very bad influence on girls like you."

"Even if they're telling the truth?" Millicent asked, partly out of mischief.

"They do not tell the truth," Mehitabel said at her most quelling. They had almost reached the door to their cabin.

"I think you had better speak to your father when you are home next summer, so that he can explain this to you more cogently."

"My father never speaks to me about serious things, except how my lessons are coming." She entered the cabin as her aunt unlocked the door.

"Then I will have to explain the circumstances to him," said Mehitabel with purpose. "Now, I want you to do something more with your hair. You've been looking like a ragamuffin, and it isn't becoming. Since you've refused to wear a proper hat, the least you can do is take care of your hair." She indicated her brushes and perfume set out for use. "It's time you began to look after yourself correctly; you're a young woman of some importance and it's fitting that you look the part."

Millicent sighed and thought of what Miss Cloris Gordon might say to such strictures.

When they reached the Grand Salon, news of the missing seaman had spread among the first-class passengers and they were bristling with speculations.

"It is a terrible thing," General Cuernos announced over the rim of his sherry glass. "It is inexcusable."

Miss Gordon, who had found a place by herself near the door, said loudly, "Is that because you deplore the occurrence or simply dislike what it may do to your convenience since the staff of servants is reduced?"

General Cuernos turned on her. "You may say what you wish, young woman; as long as you are traveling first class, your motives are questionable." His Spanish accent, which was very upper-class Castilian, caused him to lisp noticeably in English and made his reprimand sound childish, though none of the others laughed.

"Yours are so clear that there can be no question whatsoever," Miss Gordon countered.

The Emmorys, who were sitting not too far from Miss Gordon, looked up from their whispered exchange, and Mister Jared Emmory said, "From what the chief steward told us, we're the last ones to have seen that unfortunate man."

This brought silence to the room, and then an attentive buzz began. "When was that?" asked Milton Homes.

"Not too early this morning. We requested that he bring us an early luncheon in our cabin, and he did. Mister Roman, the chief steward, told us that his delivery to our cabin was the last duty logged into his records. There is nothing more they can find about the poor man." Missus Hope Emmory blushed at saying this and took her husband's hand for reassurance. "It is most disquieting."

"Don't let it trouble you, dear heart," murmured Mister Emmory, returning the pressure on her hand that she had given his.

"This is most embarrassing," whispered Mehitabel to Millicent. "Their behavior . . ."

"What was his state of mind?" demanded General Cuernos.

"He was most calm and efficient," Missus Emmory answered for them both.

"And there has been no trace of him since then?" prompted Mister Wingham.

"Not that we know of," answered Mister Emmory.

"Terrible," said one of the older passengers, a bent old man with a Dutch accent. "What a terrible thing."

Into this gloom strode the Incredible Anton, his manner open and confident. He went to the bar and ordered a sherry, then looked around at the other passengers. "What long faces you all have," he observed.

"The missing understeward," one of the passengers muttered, and this was echoed by a few other low voices.

"It was a shame about losing him overboard," Anton said affably, "but that was not recent. By the look of you, this is a more immediate problem."

"How perceptive," one of the Frenchwomen cooed in that language.

Anton bowed. "You flatter me, madame," he responded in the same.

"Sham!" said General Cuernos with contempt. "Another man is missing. But what do you care about any of this?"

"I daresay I care as much as the rest of you," Anton replied with dignity.

"Perhaps you . . ." ventured Missus Dovecote, who had arrived while the Emmorys were talking.

"Perhaps I what?" Anton asked politely. "You were about to suggest something?"

Missus Dovecote faltered. "It is only that a man of your powers should be able to be of assistance in this case."

General Cuernos snorted; Miss Gordon scoffed; Mister Homes, who was hovering in the darkest corner, looked shocked; Geoffrey Wingham gave an indulgent chuckle; Mehitabel blushed.

"Precisely," said Anton. "I am only a stage magician, not a magus or a sorcerer. What I do is illusion, and if some unfortunate man is missing, I am not able to aid you beyond volunteering to assist you in a thorough search of the ship."

"That is the first reasonable thing I have heard from you, sir," Miss Gordon declared. She rose from her seat and looked at the others in the room. "Surely the Captain or the chief steward must have a set of duplicate keys."

"A search!" exclaimed Mehitabel. "But what of the crew? Surely that is their province? Isn't the Captain supposed to tend to such matters?"

"Leave the Captain to me," said Miss Gordon emphatically, "and we can prepare to undertake the task within the hour. I am convinced that Captain Symington will share our determination to end this mystery, and if the pass keys are entrusted to"—she looked around the room and her glance settled on a rotund Dutch banker—"Mister van Vreese, there can be no doubt of his motives or his sense of responsibility. How can there be any objection?" She downed the last of her sherry with more than her usual defiance.

"Very good," said General Cuernos, in reluctant accord with a woman he wholeheartedly disapproved of. "If you can convince the Captain that this is necessary, then I am prepared to organize and lead the search." He almost saluted.

"The missing man is a foreigner," said Missus Dovecote in an undervoice. "He's from Eastern Europe somewhere." From the tone of her voice, it was clear that she was convinced that his origins had something to do with his being missing.

"Yes; I believe his name is Marek Liha," said Miss Gordon, clearly prepared for her discussion.

"It sounds Polish," said one of the elderly French passengers.

"Bohemian," corrected Anton in a soft voice.

"Same thing." The Frenchman dismissed the matter.

"Not if you are a Pole or a Bohemian," Anton said at his most suave.

"Oh, good point!" called out Mister Wingham. "You're quite the wit, Anton."

In response to this, Anton bowed. He then gave his attention to Miss Gordon. "What is your plan? I'm sure you have an excellent one."

She hesitated, as if examining his remark for hidden insults. Finding none, she said, "Assuming we obtain the Captain's approval, I propose that those who are able to participate gather here at the conclusion of dinner. We may then proceed to the various levels of the ship, where we can attempt to locate the missing man. We will work in teams, of course."

"Miss Gordon?" interjected Anton. "Since my show is stored in one of the steerage compartments, might I suggest that this be one of the first areas searched?"

"An excellent notion," approved Miss Gordon. "It will impress Captain Symington to know that you have already made this offer. I hope he will prove sympathetic to such a gesture."

Apparently Captain Symington did comply, for when dinner was over, the gathered passengers found Miss Gordon ready for them in the Grand Salon.

"We have been given three hours for our search, and Captain Symington has alerted the crew to be prepared to assist us." She consulted a notebook she carried. "And to do this most efficaciously, let me suggest that we divide into three groups." She saw that Anton was one of the passengers waiting to search. "You—Mister Anton."

"Yes?" he asked.

"If you don't mind, I'd like to assign four of this group to search the steerage level, including your storage. Since you are familiar with the way, it would be sensible for you to lead them." Miss Gordon was apparently unaware of the fuming disapproval of General Cuernos.

"I'll be delighted to assist in that way, or any other way possible." He regarded her with respect. "Do you wish me to leave now, or shall I wait until all the assignments have been made?"

"It might be wise for you to wait," said General Cuernos. "We must all commence at the same time, or there might be deception practiced."

"Whatever you prefer," said Anton, smiling briefly at Millicent, who stood not far away with her aunt.

"It might be better if he were not present while his area is searched," said General Cuernos with determination.

"Whichever you wish," said Anton. "However, some of the equipment is fragile and I would not want it to be inadvertently damaged." He let his words hang on the air for a moment, then went on. "Perhaps it would be wisest for me to be on hand, whether or not I actually take part in the search of the area."

By the time the passengers were divided up into three search parties, it was approaching ten at night. Millicent had been sternly ordered to bed, and she had ignored the command, choosing to follow Anton down to the level where his equipment was stowed.

"I thought you were supposed to be in bed," he chided her gently as they went down the companionway.

"My aunt told me to go to bed. I didn't say I would," she informed him. "Why does it matter what nationality the missing man is?"

He looked down at her. "I should have realized you'd pick up on that. It troubles me because he is a countryman of mine. You know the feeling, don't you? When you are in Europe, you pay special attention to other Americans, don't you? It is the same with me."

"Is that all of it?" she persisted, curious at how aloof he could be.

"It might not be, Millicent, but that is intruding." He held the door open for her.

"The search is intruding," she pointed out reasonably, and saw him wince.

"I'm not arguing that point; I want only to help expedite matters, so that we can return to boredom and tranquillity." He looked over his shoulder. "Here they come. Run along now."

"I think I'd rather talk to Jibben and Sabina," Millicent said with calculated determination.

"If you wish to, you'll have to wait until morning. They're both in their cabins by now, where you should be. Don't make this more difficult than it already is, if you please." He gave her a weary smile. "I'd rather talk shop with you than assist in this waste of time, but it is necessary that I cooperate. Surely you can understand that."

Millicent nodded; she did understand his predicament. "I'll talk to you tomorrow, won't I?"

"I certainly hope so," he replied, and stood back so that she could make her way out of the hold and back to the first-class level where Aunt Mehitabel and bed were waiting.

10

"This is outrageous!" thundered General Cuernos as Captain Symington ordered the body of the dead understeward covered.

"It certainly is," said Captain Symington gently. "It is also baffling. The man was alone in this closet, and the door was locked. He was shot to death, one presumes from the burns on his skin, at close range, and yet there is no appearance of a struggle, since his clothing has not been disturbed." He looked at General Cuernos. "You agree with all that, General?"

"Yes, yes, I will agree," said General Cuernos with more impatience than ever. "It is most sinister, and I, for one, believe that there are more reasons for this than chance. He did not die by misadventure."

"A man dead in a locked room can hardly be called misadventure, General," said Captain Symington curtly.

"Of course not, when there is no weapon present. If he had shot himself—"

One of the other passengers gave a shocked gasp.

"I say," the General went on in his most overbearing manner, "if this man had shot himself, then the weapon he used would be here, and we know that it is not; therefore he is the victim of a crime, and it indicates that someone aboard this ship has killed him. Think; all of you! What other conclusion is possible?" He paused to let the full effect of his words sink in. "And if there has been one murder, there may be more."

"For all we know," said Geoffrey Wingham, who was part of the group standing in the door, "the first man overboard was not an accident, either." He was looking very pale, almost greenish in tinge, as he spoke.

"That's being a bit alarmist," warned Captain Symington. "And if you are apprehensive, I suggest you take care to lock your doors. Only Chief Steward Roman and I have duplicate keys to your doors, and that should assure you. You may be correct, but I will thank you to keep your opinions to yourself."

"But surely he has made an important observation," said General Cuernos. "If there are suspicious persons aboard, they should all be confined to their quarters until we reach the first port, and then they should be turned over to the authorities for the appropriate action."

"Lock them all in irons, is that how you'd do it, General?" asked the Captain with more sternness than friendship in his manner. "Would you like to confine all the passengers while you are about it, just to be safe? Or are you limiting yourself to those you disapprove of?"

"Such measures are sensible," the General insisted, but it was apparent that he had overstepped the bounds and that those who had sympathized with him were no longer on his side.

"I will keep your suggestion in mind," said Captain Symington formally. "In the meantime, it is necessary that this body be taken to the infirmary so that the physician can examine him and prepare a report." He stepped back. "Poor fellow," he said, looking down at the shape under the blanket. "What an unfortunate ending."

General Cuernos made the sign of the cross and gave a stiff salute as the Captain strode away from them.

The four men gathered around the door exchanged uneasy looks, and finally Geoffrey Wingham said to the others, "I suppose we might as well return abovedecks. The crew will be wanting to tend to this . . . situation."

The others readily agreed, and General Cuernos made no attempt to dissuade them, choosing only to remark loudly that he was going to keep his loaded pistol under his pillow for the rest of the voyage.

By the end of breakfast, every one of the first-class passengers had been told the tale of the gruesome discovery, and the details had grown more lurid with each repetition.

"Missus Dovecote," Mehitabel said with great emotion, "do you think it would be possible for you to sit again, so soon after the last sitting? I feel that it must be in our best interests to contact the spirit world for guidance."

Auralia Dovecote, who was spooning the last of her boiled eggs onto her toast wedges, paused long enough to consider Mehitabel's request. "I think it might be possible. I am sure that you're right, Mehitabel, that it is prudent to seek the guidance of those who have passed beyond."

Mehitabel brought her hand to her bosom and turned her eyes toward the ceiling. "There are so many things in this world that confound and confuse us, it is in our best interests to find what guidance we can from those who have gone before."

"They are so much wiser than we," said Missus Dovecote, her face set in a simper.

"What utter nonsense," said a voice from the next table, and Missus Dovecote, Mehitabel, and Millicent turned to see Miss Gordon taking a sip of her coffee.

"No matter what you think, it is very bad form to speak in this way about the beliefs of other persons," said Mehitabel in what was usually a stern enough tone to make younger persons mind their manners.

"And it is worse form to be adding to the general hysteria by spouting drivel," said Miss Gordon staunchly. "You're behaving as if you *enjoy* all this upset and mischance."

"Mischance?" repeated Missus Dovecote incredulously.

"What else? You cannot seriously believe that there is some sort of plot afoot on this ship, can you?" Her very sensible eyes moved from Missus Dovecote to Mehitabel. "I see that you do have such illusions. What about you, girl?" she said, looking at Millicent.

"I think that one of the crew was murdered, and that means that whoever killed him is still aboard. But I have no idea as to why he was killed, or who did it." She folded her napkin and stood up. "I would like to be excused, please." She wanted very much to go below and have a few words with Anton.

"Not just yet, miss, if you please," said Mehitabel. "What did you mean in your last comment?"

"Only that I know nothing more than that a man was killed. It's all any of us know, really, isn't it?" She looked at the two older women and then at Miss Gordon. "If more information comes to light, then that will change things, of course."

"Very sensible," commended Miss Gordon. "You're showing more sense than those twice your age. It's one of the benefits of a proper education."

"A lot you know of it," scoffed Mehitabel, wanting to silence Miss Gordon.

"That's true," said the redoubtable Miss Gordon. "I do know a great deal about it, and I have become totally convinced that the only effective way to change the current disastrous course of the world is through the concerted efforts of educated women, which will lead to our social equality and the right to vote." She folded her arms.

"Don't be foolish, my dear," said Missus Dovecote faintly. "It's not fitting for women to vote. As to education, I will concede that in nursing and teaching the young, women have few peers, and for those vocations it is appropriate for women to be prepared for the work they will do."

"Nursing and teaching the young!" Miss Gordon jeered. "And what of literature and science and medicine? Why are those doors barred to us when they have been open to men for more than two millennia?" She was clearly about to launch into a familiar diatribe, so Millicent decided to put an end to it.

"Miss Gordon, when it is convenient, I want to talk to you about the matter of education for women. This isn't the best time or place, so perhaps later, when my aunt is busy with Missus Dovecote, I might have the chance to speak to you in your cabin?"

"I'd welcome the conversation," said Miss Gordon.

"It isn't proper," objected Mehitabel at the same time. "If you decide to do something that will disgrace your father, Millicent, I warn you, I will tell him at once of what you are doing."

"Let me find out what Miss Gordon has to say before you decide that it isn't fitting," suggested Millicent in her calmest manner. "I want to know what might be ahead of me, Aunt, don't you understand that?"

Mehitabel softened visibly under this treatment. "I do see that a young woman like you might want to have a sense of making her own way in the world. Very well, but remember that nothing you may hear from this woman or any of your teachers can have the same bearing on your choices as the suggestions of your father." She beamed at her niece and added, "If you want to be excused, you may be."

That was all Millicent was waiting for. She wished the others a good day and hurried out onto the deck.

It was almost teatime when Auralia Dovecote arrived at Mehitabel and Millicent's cabin for her third sitting. She was rigged out this time in a very pale walking gown of tiered organza in the most breathtaking shade of mauve, and she set this off with a spectacular hat. She greeted Mehitabel effusively and agreed to wait until the two gentlemen arrived before going into her trance. She was restless with anticipation. "Once I have started to commune with the spirits, I cannot resist the urge to continue," she confided to Mehitabel.

Millicent, who had remained in the room, was now told by her aunt, "It's time you ran along, Millicent. When you're older, you might want to seek guidance from the spirits of those who have gone beyond. Right now you're too young, and . . . your father might not approve." This last admission was said in an undertone, for it was closer to the truth than the rest.

"All right," said Millicent, "but when it's over, you'll have to tell me what was said." She lifted her chin and went toward the door.

"I'm sorry to have to disappoint you, Millicent," Mehitabel called after her.

"That's all right," Millicent said, taking silent delight in her aunt's discomfort. "I'll manage." Then she was out the door, almost skipping along the corridor.

"You're very sprightly, little lady," said Geoffrey Wingham as he came around the corner at the end of the hall. "It's a pity you can't join us."

Millicent did not like the way he said "little lady," but she tried to be polite. "My aunt is waiting for you and Mister Homes."

"Very good. A most amiable woman, your aunt. I've been very pleased to meet her." He gave Millicent an encouraging smile. "If she mentions me to you, you might say that I am quite taken with her."

"Why should I do that?" asked Millicent as innocently as she could. She wanted to tell the man to do his own courting, but that might lead them both to more embarrassment than either wanted. "I have to meet someone," said Millicent, stepping aside and hurrying on toward the deck.

By the time she had to change for dinner, the séance was over in the cabin and Millicent could return to it without fear of interrupting the pronouncements of Ling Lu or Big Wolf.

"It was the most remarkable thing," vowed Mehitabel as she picked up her fur wrap and draped it over her shoulders. "Big Wolf said that there are anarchists aboard—fancy that!—and they are waiting for the most opportune time to set off their bombs."

"In the middle of the Atlantic Ocean?" Millicent asked, almost smiling.

"It's no laughing matter, miss," Mehitabel rebuked her.

"But why would anyone want to bomb the ship they're sailing on? There aren't many other ships about, and there's no saying that a bomb might not be as disastrous to those setting it off as to anyone else." She had reluctantly agreed to wear her lace dress, and as always, she found herself fidgeting with it.

"Anarchists don't care for such matters," said Mehitabel in an authoritative way.

The *Duchess of Malfi* was rolling more than she had been, and the sky had turned brassy toward the horizon. Looking out the porthole, Millicent said, "I think we're going to cross another storm."

"A storm?" said Mehitabel. "Gracious, what next?"

"Probably not as bad as the other." Millicent studied the ocean and tried to remember what she had seen on her previous crossings. "I think that this one won't last as long, either."

"We'll ask the Captain about it," said Mehitabel, not

believing her niece. "And in the meantime, I want you to hold your tongue about what I've told you. Some of the others on board do not think well of spiritualism."

"Why should I talk about it? I wasn't here." Millicent took her short coat from the closet and wrapped it around her shoulders. "Besides, you and Missus Dovecote will talk about it, and I won't have to say anything."

"That's very ill-mannered, miss," Mehitabel said sharply.

Millicent knew that it was so, that she had overstepped the limits. "I didn't mean to offend you, or Missus Dovecote," she said.

"Perhaps the Incredible Anton will cheer you up; he's doing another performance tonight, isn't he?" said Mehitabel as they left their cabin.

"Yes," Millicent said, her mood lightening at the thought.

"Good. And I don't want you spending too much time with that Miss Gordon. She's a very bad example for you, since you're at a very impressionable time in your life."

Millicent wanted to know what her aunt meant by that, but she saw that Mister Wingham was approaching, and knew that further discussion would be useless.

11

"I think," said Captain Symington at the conclusion of the dinner, "that this evening's performance will have to be postponed. I need hardly say that the weather has worsened; we're all aware of it. This should not last long, but I believe that we will all enjoy the Incredible Anton more when there is less motion underfoot."

Some of the passengers laughed politely at this, but most appeared disappointed that they would not have the entertainment they had expected.

Anton rose to offer a sort of apology. "Ladies and gentlemen, it is most unfortunate, but we who live by showing you the illusions of miracles cannot, in fact, change the weather. My lovely assistant, Sabina, is very prone to seasickness, and she would not be able to perform her part correctly tonight. We would rather wait until all of us, as well as all of you, are more disposed to enjoy our presentation."

"He cannot be serious," Mehitabel said softly to Millicent. "Anyone can tell that he has it in his power to cure her seasickness. There must be another reason for his refusal."

"There is the weather," Millicent reminded her, annoyed that her aunt could think such things.

"Yes," she allowed, "but you would think that there were tricks he could do in spite of it." She folded her arms. "I think that I will retire early and read."

Millicent knew her aunt was in a huff, but she only said, "It might be that he has the passengers in mind as well as his own assistants."

"Possibly," Mehitabel said in a sinister tone.

There was no denying that the ship was rolling more, but not as dramatically as it had when the first storm had passed. This time there was a slower, almost relaxed pace to the motion of the *Duchess of Malfi,* a feeling similar to a rocking chair. A few of the passengers in the dining room looked relieved, and one of the European women said, in French, "I am very glad that I will have an evening to myself at last. And such an evening."

"Merci du compliment," said Anton with an inclination of his head. "I am devastated if I have been an imposition."

Millicent chuckled and was nudged by Mehitabel. "What are they saying?" she asked in a whisper.

"I'll tell you later," said Millicent, who noticed that there were several others who shared her amusement. It was marvelous, this feeling of being part of a special joke.

"What about a hand of whist?" suggested Geoffrey Wingham as he came to Mehitabel's side.

"Oh, I don't think so," Mehitabel declined with a look

of apology. "I am very tired, and I think that I need my rest. Another time, perhaps, Mister Wingham."

"Of course; I look forward to it." He made a point of saying good night to Millicent as well. "I'm looking forward to seeing you at breakfast, little lady."

"Thank you," Millicent said frostily.

"Why don't you like him, Millicent?" Mehitabel asked as they prepared to leave the dining room. She was watching Mister Wingham in conversation with Mister Homes. "He is a very nice man."

"I know you like him, Aunt," said Millicent. "He's trying very hard to make you like him."

"What?" Mehitabel said in surprise. "Are you afraid that he's a fortune hunter? Why, he's making a grave mistake—I have no fortune at all." She smiled, her reassurance apparent. "You don't have to worry on that account. I haven't more than the clothes on my back."

But your brother has, thought Millicent, and he would not allow you to live like a church mouse. She kept her opinions to herself, wanting to be certain of Mister Wingham before she spoke to her aunt about her suspicions. "I think he does like you, and that's something," she said honestly as they went through the Grand Salon.

Just before they went out, Mehitabel turned back to wave at Mister Wingham, who was sitting down to a rubber of whist with a sallow-faced merchant from Liège, Mister Homes, and Miss Gordon. She was rewarded with a return wave from Mister Wingham, and then she and Millicent were through the doors and on their way down the corridor to their cabin.

Mehitabel was ready for bed in less than thirty minutes, but Millicent, once she had got out of her lace dress, wrapped herself in her dressing gown and sat in the parlor, reading. Her mind was restless, and she could not bring herself to sleepiness. She went so far as to read her book on mathematical puzzles, which only irritated her but did not make her eyes droop. The steady rocking of the ship was not soothing, as she had expected it might be, and finally she rose and changed into her warmest walking dress, took her serge coat from the closet, and decided that she would have a brisk turn around the deck. She had done this before on her other crossings, and it had worked most of the time. Checking to be sure that Mehitabel was asleep, Millicent took the key and went out the door, securing it behind her.

There was a gray, clinging mist shrouding the ship, and the sound of the water against the hull was like a long series of heavy sighs. Millicent set herself a quick pace as she started down the deck, hearing the crisp sound of her shoes as steady as the ticking of a clock.

She had rounded the fantail deck when she heard a sound near the companionway to the bridge, and she paused, feeling a touch of apprehension that she did not want to admit. It galled her to think that she could be easily frightened.

There were other footsteps, and then a figure swam out of the fog. "It's very late for you to be up, isn't it?" asked Anton.

Millicent sighed. "If it's late for me, then it's late for you as well," she said, waiting for him to come up to her. "What are you doing out in this weather?"

"I might ask you the same thing, but I assume that your aunt and the redoubtable Missus Dovecote are summoning the spirits for the latest bulletins." He sounded slightly bitter, but not angry. With a nod, he started to walk, Millicent beside him.

"No, they aren't. Actually, my aunt is asleep. I'm too wide awake to go to bed yet, and so I decided to get some exercise."

"Does that mean you and your aunt have quarreled?" asked Anton with genuine curiosity.

"No. We don't quarrel. Aunt Mehitabel never quarrels with anyone, ever. It's one of the things that bothers me about her." She fixed her eyes on an imaginary spot about three feet ahead of her stride.

"Poor woman," said Anton.

Millicent nodded. "My father always praises her for being tractable, but . . . I don't want to have to be like that. My aunt is a good woman, I know, and I'm probably not going to be as good, but when I think about her, I know I'd rather do almost anything than be like her, no matter how nice she is." She swallowed hard and waited for the reprimand she was certain would follow her admission.

"I can't say that I blame you," Anton remarked. "But don't you ever feel sorry for her?"

"*Always,*" Millicent said with feeling. "And that's what makes it worse. I never want anyone to feel so sorry for me."

"Ah, it's a matter of pride, then." He clearly did not expect her to respond, but was silent in case she wanted to.

"In part," she confessed. "I'm afraid to be like her, too. She's got nowhere to go."

"That's very sad," Anton said.

"It is. And sometimes I think it makes her sillier than she is. When she's around my father, she's like a puppy, adorable and helpless and fawning, and it disgusts me."

"You're very severe," Anton observed.

"I know, and I wish I weren't," she told him. "I try to understand, but sometimes it's just too hard." She set her jaw and deliberately changed the subject. "I was sorry about the performance."

"Sorry?" he asked, raising a quizzical eyebrow, then went on. "So was I, but Sabina was delighted. It seems that she has some new beau who wanted a little of her time this evening, and if she were being run through with spikes in the Iron Maiden, she couldn't have an hour or so with him." He had lit one of his long, thin cheroots, and the end of it glowed like a tame firefly just beyond his fingers, reminding Millicent of some of his illusions.

"She isn't really run through with spikes, is she?"

"It certainly looks as if she is—what do you think?" He waited for her answer.

"I think that's what it *looks* like." She spoke very carefully, not wanting to be misunderstood.

"But?" he prompted.

"But if she were run through, that would kill her, and so, obviously, she isn't and there is a trick to it, an illusion." She did her best to appear matter-of-fact.

"Very good," Anton said, but although he had his usual air of encouragement, it was apparent that his thoughts were now mildly distracted.

"Is something wrong?" Millicent ventured to ask when they had walked a little way in silence.

He looked down at her, considering his answer. "I'm tempted to say no. It is what I ought to say. At any other hour, it is definitely what I *would* say. However, the correct answer is yes, something is wrong." He drew on his cheroot and went on. "But it is nothing new, and it has nothing to do with you, or, in fact, with this ship or the performances."

"What is it?" The thought of sharing confidences with this intriguing man gave Millicent a tremendous sense of pride. Someone was finally treating her like an adult, and letting her be truly grown-up.

"Actually, I've been thinking about my childhood," said Anton reflectively and sadly. "I suppose going back to Europe has triggered more than I thought it would."

"Bohemia!" exclaimed Millicent, recalling what he had said earlier.

"That's right," he said. "Bohemia. June 24, 1867, when the Erzherzog Ulric Tancred Ambroz was born—I was thinking about that."

"Forty-three years ago," Millicent said promptly. "Why is that Bohemian archduke"—she was very glad she had learned that an erzherzog was the same as an archduke—"so important?"

"He isn't, anymore," Anton said whimsically. "Most of the time, I hardly remember him at all. But every now and then, he comes back to haunt me." He strolled along with her, saying nothing more for a quarter the length of the deck.

"Why?" Millicent dared to ask at last.

Anton stopped and looked down at her. "I don't think we should be talking about this."

"Why not?" she demanded. "You're the one who started it." She was angry for the way he was treating her, one moment like an adult, the next like a child. "If you tell me not to repeat what you say, I won't. I'm very good at that." It was true, she decided. Each of her parents was always giving her long lists of things she was not to tell the other. Most of the time she did as they asked.

"I don't doubt that, Millicent. You're a very self-reliant child. That's why I like you: your self-reliance and your intelligence. In some ways, you remind me of myself." He laughed once. "What terrible vanity."

"You think that I'm like you?" Millicent wondered, so pleased that she could think of no way to thank him.

"In some ways. The trappings are different but the circumstances are similar, I think." They walked on a little farther. "Each of us was cast adrift young. Oh, not like the urchins and orphans in the streets, or the miserable little wretches in the mills and mines, but in another way. You have half your family in America and the other half in Europe, and unless I miss my guess, you are the only link between the two."

Millicent swallowed and her eyes stung. "Yes," she said softly, realizing that if she expected him to confide in her, she would have to confide in him.

"The Emperor called my mother and the four of us to Vienna, supposedly as an honor to the family, but, of course, he wanted to keep my father in line. It guaranteed his cooperation if his wife and family were honored hostages. Not that there was any real cause for concern: Bohemia was long lost by then, and only a few fanatics thought otherwise." His face clouded. "Fanatics. They were still with us when I was young. I suppose there are some left even now."

Millicent remembered something that Sabina had said to Anton, and his answer—something about his father and uncle and three brothers being killed by a mob. "They . . . killed your father?"

"And my uncle and my brothers," he said. "I wondered if you'd heard that. I'm not often so careless, and Jibben warned me that you have a keen wit."

"Why did they do that? What was the reason?" Millicent asked, horrified and fascinated at once.

"I said, they were fanatics. I'm not really sure what the issue was. I was quite young, and I didn't understand what was going on. I was almost nine; the oldest. My father and his brother had my brothers with them because they were allowed to attend those sorts of celebrations. Mama and I were permitted to watch, but in the company of the Emperor's Guard. From what I remember, there was a group of men in striped jackets who interrupted the ceremony, and then a riot started. Mama and I were taken to the inner part of the castle, and then put into a sealed coach bound for Vienna. Mama cried all the way." His voice had become remote, and he had let his cheroot fall from his fingers. "I saw them stoning my family, shouting and cursing, and I remember seeing the soldiers fire into the crowd. When I was younger, I had nightmares about it."

"And why is the birth of the Erzherzog so important?" asked Millicent, not wanting to make assumptions that seemed wild to her, but determined to find out if her guess, no matter how outlandish, was correct. She could not help hoping that it was.

"Because, as you have probably figured out, June 24, 1867, is when I was born." He spoke quietly and rather slowly. "Ulric Tancred Ambroz. There are three or four saints' names after that, and then all the nobility, but my own name, without the rest, was Ulric Tancred Ambroz. Mama called me Tancred. I used to think it was dreadful."

"So *that* was what it meant," Millicent said, enthralled at what he had told her. "I wondered why Sabina called you 'Duke.' "

"She only does when she is very angry with me. She resents my title, though it's no longer mine." He stared into the fog. "That was a long time ago. I abdicated any claims to title or privilege before . . . oh, long before it might have mattered. I signed a provisional abdication when I was thirteen, and a formal one when I reached my majority."

"Does that bother you, that you gave it all up?" Millicent wanted to know, for she could sense no rancor in him.

"Good heavens, no," Anton said with a snort of laughter. "I was glad to be shut of the filthy business. The best I could have been as a duchyless archduke was a political pawn. I much prefer being the Incredible Anton to being a hounded and penniless nobleman in an empire that's headed toward revolution."

"Revolution?" Millicent said, astonished, since none of her teachers had ever hinted at such a possibility.

"Revolution or war. Either way, I'm well out of it." He sighed, but not unhappily. "It was very hard, being Tancred; it's wonderfully easy to be Anton. And as Anton, at least I provide some entertainment, some amusement, and I am able to live fairly much as I like. I am my own man, and that is worth a great deal to me. It is something that would never be possible for Tancred, poor boy."

"You make him sound like another person," Millicent said, more curious than ever.

"There are times he seems that way. I remember those days as if they had happened to someone else." He let his words drift away. "I don't suppose you can understand. You're—what?—thirteen or fourteen?"

"Fourteen," Millicent said with all her dignity.

"Well, in 1939, if you remember to, think back to this conversation and see if you feel then as you feel now. You'll probably think of yourself as a different person living in a different world. You'll be my age then, and you'll . . ." He did not finish.

"I hate it when everyone tells me that I'll understand when I'm older," Millicent said with vehemence. "Why do I have to wait until I'm older? What makes you think I can't understand this now? I do know that I see things very differently now than I did when I was six, and that's the same thing, isn't it?"

"I suppose so," he conceded. "I didn't mean to offend you, Millicent."

"I'm not very offended," she said quickly, so that he could not accuse her of being childish. She decided to change this dangerous subject. "When did you become the Incredible Anton? Was it long after you . . . abdicated?"

He looked reflectively at the fog-fuzzy line of the ship's railing. "Actually, it was long before. I started doing card tricks when I was a boy." He looked down at his large, flexible hands. "My brothers liked them, and later on it was something I could do that no one minded. I did more card tricks and rope tricks and tricks with glasses and cups. It seemed the most natural thing in the world to keep expanding. By the time I was seventeen, I had done a few stage performances, and I liked doing them."

"Oh," said Millicent, who had hoped that his choice had come about more dramatically.

Anton put his hands in his pockets. "It's chilly out."

"That's why I wore my coat," Millicent said, walking along beside him and trying not to yawn.

"Millicent . . ." Anton said when they had gone a little farther, "I would prefer it if you didn't mention any of this to your aunt."

"I said I wouldn't tell anyone," Millicent reminded him sharply.

"Yes; I appreciate that. It's not as if this is a life-and-death secret, but in general, I'd rather it not be known; all right?" He was diffident as he said this, looking down at the toes of his shoes as they walked. "Sometimes it's awkward to have . . ."

"I won't tell anyone," Millicent repeated.

"All right," Anton said. "I'm not asking for a blood oath, mind; just a little good sense, and you have plenty of that." He stopped, reached up in a stretch. "You must be exhausted."

"I'm fine," Millicent said, feeling sleepier by the minute.

Anton had taken his watch from his pocket. "Lord, it's after midnight. Both of us ought to be asleep." He took her by the elbow. "Come on; I'll escort you back to your cabin."

"You don't have to," Millicent protested.

"Millicent, it is the least I can do." He was not going to argue with her, and she did not want to protest too much.

"I'm glad you told me," she said as she fumbled for the key in her pocket as they stood outside her cabin.

"Are you?" Anton said, thoughtfully. "Then so am I."

12

When they forced the door to his cabin open, they found Geoffrey Wingham crumpled beside the unmade bed. He was still in his evening dress, although his dinner jacket lay on the overturned chair and his cuff links were on the washstand. The cord was fixed deeply around his neck; his face was swollen and the color of blue plums. A single bright spangle was caught in his fingers.

"Somebody bring the Captain!" ordered Chief Steward Roman as he staggered back from the sight. "And call some of the crew to assist us. We will need the physician at once."

Those with him scurried to do his bidding, one of them turning pale at what he had seen.

General Cuernos, who stood beside Vaclav Roman, nodded several times. "You see? You see? It is precisely as I've said. There is someone aboard who is determined to murder us all."

"This isn't a natural death," the chief steward said, stating the obvious, as he moved out of the cabin and half closed the door.

"There must be more stringent methods. We must confine all suspicious persons at once!" He shouted this last.

"This ship isn't a parade ground, sir, if you'll excuse me for saying so," said the chief steward, his accent growing stronger. "I take my orders from Captain Symington. If you have something you want done, you'll have to ask the Captain to do it."

"You may be sure that I will," said the General, and turned to see Milton Homes standing not far away. "There's been another killing," he said bluntly.

"I see," said Mister Homes, hunching over more than usual. "We were playing whist last night, Mister Wingham and I." He cleared his throat. "I missed him at breakfast." For Mister Homes, this was a great deal of talking.

"Perhaps he should have played longer," said the General with harsh humor.

"I must request that both you passengers leave the area until Captain Symington can decide what to do," Chief Steward Roman said to Mister Homes and General Cuernos.

"I assisted in this!" protested General Cuernos.

"I'm sure the Captain is looking forward to discussing it with you," said the chief steward, showing no inclination to give ground to the General.

"You will figure in my remarks," threatened the General as he turned away. "You can count on it."

"How did you find him?" asked Mister Homes as he and the General went down the narrow hallway.

General Cuernos was still sputtering with rage and he

grew flushed as he spoke. "We had to force the door. It was locked. You saw where the man had fallen. You see what he grasps in his hand. We found him there. That pig of a steward will be reprimanded for his actions, be certain of it."

"Was there any sign of a struggle?" asked Mister Homes, tucking his head farther between his lean shoulders.

"The man was strangled. He must have struggled. The room was disarranged, if that is your meaning." He stopped walking and peered at Mister Homes. "You are asking a great many questions."

"I am worried," mumbled Mister Homes, avoiding the piercing glance of the General.

"Naturally," said the General with scorn as he strode ahead of the self-effacing Mister Milton Homes.

Long before the Captain made a formal announcement to the passengers, news of Mister Wingham's death had spread through all those in first class.

"Oh!" cried Mehitabel when Missus Dovecote informed her of the event. "Not Mister Wingham!"

Millicent, who was sitting in the deck chair next to her aunt's, looked up, alarmed at what she heard.

"I know it must prostrate you, but I felt I must tell you before some less sympathetic person should inform you," Missus Dovecote exclaimed. "Mehitabel, you're very pale. Shall I order a tot of brandy to restore you?"

"I . . . shouldn't drink spirits," Mehitabel said faintly. She was trying to take a deep breath without success. "Oh, dear, I wish I had not done my corsets so firmly."

"Are you well?" Missus Dovecote asked, taking Mehitabel's hand in hers and patting it. "Are you sure you're going to be all right?"

"Mister Wingham was killed?" Millicent asked, looking at Missus Dovecote with curiosity and doubt.

"They found him this morning. Strangled." She at once turned to Mehitabel. "I'm so sorry to be the one to tell you, but you had to learn of it within the hour."

"Auralia," said Mehitabel, "you say he was strangled?"

"I have heard that the fatal cord was still around his neck. It is really most tragic. Such a pleasant, well-mannered man." She continued to regard Mehitabel closely. "Please, come inside. You need a little time to compose yourself. I cannot tell you how distressed I am, Mehitabel."

Millicent's aunt got unsteadily to her feet; her complexion, under the brightness from the wind, was chalky. "Thank you," she said softly. "I would appreciate that, Auralia."

"You needn't accompany us, Millicent," said Missus Dovecote as she assisted Mehitabel to walk down the deck. "At times like these, a grown woman knows what's best for another grown woman. If you want company, there are others in the Grand Salon. No doubt it will be all right for you to go there."

"I might," said Millicent, feeling disappointed that she was being excluded, for little as she liked Mehitabel's airs and manner, she was fond of her aunt and knew that she was very upset. She watched the two women as they went indoors, and then tried to return to her reading. She tried to concentrate on the trials that Richardson's virtuous Pamela endured, but her thoughts would not remain with the book. She kept being distracted by images of Mister Wingham and his ready smile. While Millicent did not try to convince herself that she had liked the man, she certainly was not able to be unmoved by his death, and by her aunt's distress. Why on earth, she asked herself, would anyone want to kill a man like Mister Wingham? It made more sense to want to kill Captain Symington, or General Cuernos, or even Anton, for that matter—but Geoffrey Wingham? Who else might die? She closed her book and got up, strolling toward the Grand Salon as she started to think.

Quite a number of the first-class passengers were in the Grand Salon, and for once the mood was subdued. One couple, middle-aged and French, were talking earnestly with General Cuernos, their voices lowered but emphatic. As Millicent sat down, she listened closely and hoped that they were not aware that she understood them.

"The Captain should confine all questionable persons at once," said the General in his very Spanish French, harping on his favorite theme.

"Yes; yes; a sensible thing to do."

"Then I and a few officers could organize a patrol of the corridors and decks to be continued until we reach port. It is essential that we restore the confidence of the passengers as well as find out who the dastard is who is committing these heinous crimes." General Cuernos grew adamant.

"Whoever this person is, he can walk through walls," said the Frenchman with condemnation apparent in every aspect of his posture and voice.

"Like our magician," quipped his wife, who was showing signs of being worried about the General.

General Cuernos turned toward her. "Precisely. And that fop Wingham was holding a spangle when we found him."

"General, it was merely a joke," said the helpless woman as she tugged at her husband's arm.

"Much truth is spoken in jest. Each of us is custodian of the key to his quarters and only the Captain and the chief steward have duplicates; they certainly are above question, and so we are looking for someone who can penetrate locked doors. The man killing passengers works miracles. From his success, it is not too preposterous to assume that he is almost invisible." General Cuernos paused dramatically. "It is very like the magician, who flaunts just such skills for our entertainment."

Millicent was horrified. She wanted to protest, but if she did, she would reveal that she had been listening, and that she had a good command of French. It seemed to her that if she could continue the pretense, she might learn more. It was an effort to keep her expression bland and slightly bored.

"I will discuss this with the Captain at once. He must be alerted," declared General Cuernos. "He can take action as soon as I explain our thoughts to him."

"General, you yourself have said repeatedly that you think the man is nothing more than a charlatan," the Frenchman reminded him in a desperate attempt at humoring him.

"Yes, I have, which shows how clever he is. What more effective way to go about his work than to have us all think he is nothing more than a buffoon?" General Cuernos's eyes narrowed. "He is trying to deceive us all, and in more ways than one," he said.

"For heaven's sake, General," the Frenchman objected.

"I applaud him for his cleverness. He had me fooled for a time, but now he is going too far, and I have discovered his secret. He is going to regret his work on this ship, I promise you." He was already starting toward the door when Miss Gordon rose before him. "Out of my way, woman!"

"Why? So that you can go to Captain Symington and make a difficult matter worse? So that you can accuse an entertainer or sham, as you say he is, of being a murderer? Does it make you feel better to think that the man you have decided has done the killing is not one of those you approve of? You have been determined to find a way to discredit the Incredible Anton since you saw his first performance, and you have at last hit upon a way." She folded her arms, apparently unaware of all the attention they had attracted.

"Stand aside!" ordered the General.

"I think not, General. You may want to take up the Captain's time with this folly, but I would prefer he spend his time tending to the ship and the hunting out of the real villains." Her face was calm but her voice rang.

"You know nothing of these matters," the General raged at her.

"True enough, and neither do you." She glanced around the room for the first time. "You are an officer, not a policeman."

The dart stuck. If there was one thing that General Cuernos could not endure, it was being compared to what he felt were inferior persons. "A policeman!"

"That's what we need in this case, or a good detective." Miss Gordon looked around the room again. "And since none of us is either, I suggest that we let the Captain handle the matter as best he can, and that we do not interfere with his work."

This time there was some support for her suggestions. One of the British passengers even went so far as to say, "Bravo, old girl," to Miss Gordon for taking matters in hand.

"The Captain will feel differently, I warn you," said the General. "He will welcome my assistance."

"That's more bluster than fact," said Miss Gordon, stepping aside at last.

"You are the most unfeminine creature ever to wear skirts," the General thundered at her, his face darkening.

"For me, that is a compliment, and I thank you." She returned to her seat, the lingering traces of a smile on her lips.

Milton Homes, who had watched most of this, now said in a low and shaky voice, "Still, you never know. There is something uncanny about that magician." Then he looked around, startled. "I'm sorry," he said to the room at large. "I didn't realize I was speaking aloud." With that, he took the mug he had been drinking from and hurried out of the room, his shoulders hunched more than ever.

"Ridiculous!" said Miss Gordon.

"Who can be sure?" said one of the passengers from Scandinavia. "There is something remarkable about the man."

"He's a performer," said Miss Gordon, both as an explanation and as a dismissal. "He's supposed to make you feel that way."

Millicent added in a voice that sounded very loud to her own ears, "He's an illusionist. He does tricks, that's all."

"The girl's right," one of the British passengers said

firmly. "And if a child realizes that, then the rest of us should be able to keep it in mind."

"An excellent cover for other activities," snapped the General as he stormed out the door.

"He wants to believe the worst," said Miss Gordon to the room. "Especially if it adds to his importance."

One of the passengers chuckled; another gave a strangled bleat of laughter. The worst of the moment had passed.

"It's too bad that your friend should be such a target," said Miss Gordon as she rose and came over to Millicent's small table.

"My friend?" asked Millicent with her most inoffensive air. Most of the time it distracted adults, but Miss Gordon was not to be put off.

"Oh, come, Millicent; you and Anton have become great friends, haven't you? He talks to you, and I understand you have even been permitted to see the props for his show. You certainly know better than the rest of us what he can and cannot do." She smiled, her manner frank and amiable. "I'm glad you have such good sense. Most girls your age are not so fortunate."

Millicent did not know what to say in answer to this. "I do like Anton," she said finally. "He's interesting."

"An accolade, believe me," said Miss Gordon. "And one that says a great deal about the both of you." She looked up. "Would you like to share tea with me?"

"Oh, yes, please," said Millicent, trying very hard not to grin, since she was afraid that if she did, she might appear to be too young and would lose the ground she had gained with the formidable Miss Cloris Gordon.

"Fine," said Miss Gordon with a smile of her own. "We can be two sensible women together in this sea of credulity." With that, she signaled for one of the waiters and gave her order in her usual brisk style, adding to Millicent, "They aren't used to taking orders from women, unless they are older and plainly established. This is one of the many things that we must work to change."

Millicent heard the *we* and was pleased to be included, although she was not certain what she might do that would alter such things. She hesitated to mention this, not wanting to offend Miss Gordon. "Do you think they'll bring us scones with the tea?"

"They usually do," said Miss Gordon. "Now, I want you to tell me what you are studying at school and what you plan to do with your education."

"Well," said Millicent, a bit startled, "I hadn't thought that far ahead."

"You ought to," said Miss Gordon. "The time will be upon you before you know it, and then you will have to be prepared. You say that you have studied languages and some sciences: have you considered such work?" She was very businesslike now, reminding Millicent of her athletic instructor who insisted that her girls play as hard as boys.

"I suppose I never thought that it would be soon," said Millicent. "I think that perhaps . . . whatever I do, I would like to travel while doing it. I've traveled so much, you see." She put her head to one side as she considered further. "I don't think I want to be a teacher." She knew that her father would never permit her to do such a thing, and for the first time she wondered what plans he might have for her himself.

"Do not let anyone deter you from what you wish to do," advised Miss Gordon, as if reading Millicent's mind. "You need to make decisions for yourself." With that, she changed the subject once again. "You ought to inform your magician friend of what is being said, no matter how irresponsible it may be, so that he will not find himself in embarrassing situations with some of the other passengers."

"Yes," said Millicent. "I planned to do that."

"Very good," approved Miss Gordon. "And here is the tea; they even remembered the scones."

13

At breakfast the following morning, the passengers chattered nervously, and one of them insisted on describing how amazed she had been during the performance of the Incredible Anton the night before when he had escaped from the chains and padlocks that had apparently secured him to a chair.

"I know for a fact," the woman hooted, "that he could not have got out any way but a magical one. He may say it is an illusion if he likes, but I touched those chains and the padlocks, and they are quite solid."

"And the Iron Maiden. That was miraculous. There was no way his assistant could have escaped from the spikes, and the marks on her dress showed that they passed right through her. How was that done, answer me that?" The elderly man at her side was quite belligerent as he spoke, as if asking someone to argue with him.

Milton Homes, who was huddled over his bacon and eggs, suddenly raised his head. "He frightens me," he said to no one in particular. "Last night, after the performance, while I was preparing for bed, I thought there was a dark presence in my cabin and something seemed to close about my throat. I tried to convince myself it was not Anton, that I was merely impressed with what he had done on the stage, but this morning I found a spangle by my bed, the same sort of spangle that Mister Wingham had in his hand, the same sort of spangle the magician's assistant wears on her costumes."

This created a sensation, and many of those seated at the table expressed shock and amazement.

"You might have found it after the performance," one of the passengers suggested.

"And it stuck to my clothing? Perhaps," said Milton Homes, now made awkward by the attention he had attracted.

Mehitabel, pale and subdued, nudged Millicent. "You will not say that Mister Homes is fanciful; he is too meek to want to call himself to general notice, and yet—"

Millicent shook her head, trying to conceal the fear she felt for her friend. "It's silly," she insisted. "Mister Homes is frightened of everything, and now he's decided to be frightened of Anton because of a spangle that Anton doesn't even wear." It was a weak defense and she knew it, but it was the best she could invent without warning.

"That is not very respectful toward Mister Homes," Mehitabel rebuked her niece. "I want you to think about what you've said, and then you can tell me you have become less stringent in your judgments, miss."

"But he always looks as if he's frightened," protested Millicent, startled that her aunt would take such an attitude. "You said so yourself."

"That was under different circumstances. No one had been hurt. No one had . . . died." She put her hand to her temple. "I knew from the first that this voyage would not go well. I sensed that there would be disasters."

"Aunt Mehitabel!" said Millicent, shocked.

"I concealed it from you and your father, of course," said Mehitabel, "and I hoped for the best, but I see now that I should have paid more attention."

This was more than Millicent could accept. "For two months all you've talked about was how much you looked forward to traveling and how you knew that the voyage would be delightful. You said you wanted to come more than anything." She sipped her milk and watched her aunt. "Was all of that for Father's benefit?"

"Most of it," said Mehitabel with dignity. "And I didn't want to worry you."

"Yet you said nothing about your premonitions? Are you certain you had them, or did you just suffer from traveler's nerves?" Millicent had seen her aunt spend four days packing, and she was convinced that her premonitions were a convenient fiction.

"I did," she insisted. "I didn't want to mention them to Haywood, in case he should change his mind about the journey."

"The premonitions couldn't have been that bad, then," said Millicent with finality. "You would have said something if they were really serious."

Mehitabel did not deign to answer her. She picked at her food and sighed.

Milton Homes finished his breakfast and got up, saying in an undervoice, "The magician is malignant, that's all I can think. He's evil, and he tries to disguise it with entertainments."

"Bosh," said Miss Gordon, who had overheard him. "You're as bad as General Cuernos."

"What?" Milton Homes gave a startled jump.

"I think that you're letting yourself be persuaded by your own fear, Mister Homes," said Miss Gordon at her briskest. "You are trying to find someone to blame for your fright."

"And you're *not* afraid?" he countered.

"Of course I'm . . . concerned," she said. "When such terrible things happen, any sensible person is worried. But I do not need a scapegoat on whom to fix my fears, as you appear to." She was able to put a degree of contempt into her politeness that barely escaped being insulting.

"Say what you will," growled Mister Homes. "The man is dangerous, and you cannot convince me otherwise."

"You're being childish," said Miss Gordon, summing up her feelings on the matter.

"I'm glad she said that," Millicent told Mehitabel softly. "It's ridiculous to think that Anton could do anything like . . . kill anyone."

"And what would you know about it? You're dazzled by him." Mehitabel sniffed.

"I'm not dazzled by him," said Millicent, almost laughing. "There might be others who are, but I'm not. He's not the sort of man who would want to kill anyone, especially someone like Mister Wingham, or a few crew members. What good would it do him?"

"Auralia told me that those who worship the devil don't need a reason to kill. It might be that to do his tricks, he has to make an offering of some kind, and these murders are his offering." Mehitabel took her napkin and dabbed at the corners of her mouth.

"Rubbish," said Millicent, ignoring the condemning look her aunt gave her. "If he was like that—and he's not—he'd have to be very stupid to go around making victims of other passengers. It makes no sense."

"If you cannot mind your manners, miss, we have nothing more to say," Mehitabel informed Millicent as she got up from the table.

The day passed slowly, many of the passengers choosing to keep to their quarters rather than spend time speculating about the additional frights of the last days. Mehitabel sought out Auralia Dovecote and the two women passed most of the afternoon in deep conversation on the problems of widows and women with invalid husbands. Millicent found little to occupy herself and at last went down to Anton's hold where his show was stored, hoping to find the magician.

He was in his shirt sleeves, working on the back panel of a large box. "It still squeaks," he said to Jibben as Millicent came through the door.

"I can't do more without taking off the back entirely," he said to Anton. "The release is bent a little; that's the problem."

Anton stood up, then caught sight of Millicent. "Hello," he said to her. "Come in."

"You weren't at breakfast or lunch," she said to him, "so I decided I'd have to come and talk to you here."

"Good," he said with a trace of a smile. "We've been

trying to get the Spirit Cabinet to work properly for most of the morning. Jibben has done all that he can, and I think that it's going to have to keep until we land." He ran a hand over his hair. "I wish I had thought to order lunch. I'm getting hungry."

"They're saying strange things about you," Millicent warned him, finding no way to break the news to him gently.

Anton sighed. "I suppose I ought to expect it. Do they think I'm responsible for the murders, is that it?"

"Some people seem to think you are," she said. "Others don't. They're silly."

"No, they're frightened," Anton corrected her gently. "They are trapped on this ship, with almost nothing to do but eat and sleep and speculate, and someone is killing men on this ship." He signaled to Jibben. "Tell Sabina that we won't have to rehearse until this evening. Captain Symington said that he wants to postpone our performance for a night, so that will give her time with her new beau, whoever he is."

Jibben nodded, watching Millicent covertly. "I'll do it."

"Thanks," Anton said. "Apparently you don't think I'm the one responsible for the deaths," he went on to Millicent.

"Of course not. You'd have to be very stupid to kill people that way." She folded her arms. "There are some very idiotic people on this ship."

Anton chuckled. "Luckily, you're not one of them. I'm glad of that."

"You're my friend," said Millicent staunchly. "It makes me very angry to hear some of the others say the things they do about you."

"Thank you," said Anton. "I hope you're not the only one who feels that way."

"Miss Gordon said Mister Homes's fear was bosh," Millicent recalled with relish. "It *was* bosh."

"Even Milton Homes thinks I had something to do with the death of Mister Wingham?" He frowned. "I thought the two of them talked . . ." He stopped. "They were at your aunt's séances, weren't they? Perhaps Mister Homes is more credulous than I thought he was."

"He's foolish," Millicent said, feeling her annoyance grow strong again.

"Be careful with fools, Millicent, especially when they are frightened. They're the ones who lash out without any consideration or understanding." He rolled down his sleeves as he spoke and looked around the hold. "I was hoping that some of those misapprehensions had ended."

"I'll do what I can," said Millicent, not sure what it might be that she could do, but determined to be of some help to Anton.

He smiled at her. "I appreciate that; I really do."

"And I'll try to get my aunt to stop being so silly," she went on with determination.

"You and the redoubtable Miss Gordon," said Anton. "You make a formidable pair."

Millicent looked hard at Anton, suspecting that he was teasing her. "Well, we are," she said defensively.

"Yes; I agree," Anton told her, his eyes tired, their tawny color faded almost to tan.

"What's the matter?" Millicent got up the courage to ask.

"I'm worried," he said frankly. "I tell myself that there is no reason to be, then everything comes back to me, and

I—" He stopped abruptly, rubbing his hand over his jaw. "First the understeward and then Mister Wingham. And possibly the man overboard. What is the point of it? Nothing makes sense."

"It probably does to whoever is doing the killing," said Millicent.

"Such a very sensible girl," sighed Anton. "And undoubtedly you're right. If there were a way to discover the sense of it, then it follows that the culprit would make himself—or herself—plain. You remind me of Doyle's Sherlock Holmes."

Millicent giggled, then felt she had to explain. "When you said 'Holmes,' I was thinking of Mister Homes, and was trying to picture him as a great detective. It was funny."

Anton nodded once. "I see your point."

Yet Millicent frowned as he spoke. "The odd thing is, I can imagine he might do strange things, sometimes. There's something about him that I don't understand, and that bothers me."

"Don't waste your time," Anton suggested. "General Cuernos is much more important just now than Milton Homes."

"General Cuernos is dreadful," Millicent proclaimed.

"Absolutely; and he's searching for a worthy victim of his fear. That makes him very dangerous." Anton gazed across the room. "The Incredible Anton is perfect for his purposes. He wouldn't dream of suspecting an archduke, even an abdicated one." He turned away from her. "There are a dozen magicians with self-invested titles performing on stages all over the world. They amuse me. General Cuernos troubles me."

"Are you frightened?" asked Millicent with less confidence than at first.

"Yes. I would be foolish not to be." He took a deep breath. "Don't let's go on about it. You have lessons to do and I have two more of these props to inspect. The constant movement of the ship is very hard on them."

"I wondered about that," Millicent said, grateful for this new subject.

"Of course you did. So leave me to these chores. I want to have all my equipment in good form when we land. Taking care of these inspections often lasts all day." He indicated the door. "Off you go. We'll talk again later; I promise."

"Good," she said to him, heading to the door obediently. "It helps to have a friend to talk to."

"It certainly does," Anton said, waving as she left the hold.

By the time Millicent returned to her cabin, she was lost in a thoughtful silence. She did not want to talk to her aunt and Missus Dovecote, who were huddled together over the tea things.

"Goodness, thank heaven you're back," Mehitabel exclaimed as Millicent closed the door and looked for the book she had been reading.

"I was talking with Anton," Millicent said.

"That terrible man!" Missus Dovecote burst out, looking shocked.

"He's my friend, Missus Dovecote," Millicent said as politely as she could.

"Oh, don't be so severe," Mehitabel reprimanded her niece. "Auralia is only concerned for your safety and well-being. As long as there are crew members about, we are doubtless all safe, but it would be senseless to remain alone on any part of the ship. Take care to be in view of the stewards and you will be safe. That includes the time you spend with the magician. You are letting yourself be mesmerized by that . . . person!"

"He's my friend, Aunt Mehitabel," Millicent repeated. "He isn't terrible and there's no reason to worry about my safety with him. I'm in no danger from Anton."

Missus Dovecote gave her a pitying look. "It's very good of you to defend your friends, Millicent, but for such defense, they must be worthy of your friendship, and there are many excellent reasons to believe that this man is not worthy of your concern. He is simply taking advantage of your gullibility and naïveté, and puffing up his own tawdry fame to impress you. Your aunt's warnings are well taken, and if you are as sensible a girl as she says you are, you will heed them."

"Why do you say this?" Millicent asked, trying to keep from becoming angry. "You've been listening to those silly passengers in the Grand Salon who have nothing better to do than sip sherry all day long and gossip about everyone. You think that General Cuernos, because he wears a uniform and struts and shouts, has better sense than anyone else."

Both Mehitabel and Missus Dovecote shrank from this outburst, and they looked at each other in deep concern.

"Oh, dear, I don't suppose there's any way to tell you this; that is . . . You do understand that . . ." Mehitabel lost herself in a tangle of half-thoughts.

"Tell me what?" Millicent asked, hoping that the two women would not lecture her anymore.

"It's General Cuernos," Missus Dovecote said with difficulty. "They found him hanging in his room not half an hour ago." Her hand fluttered to her bosom and she gave a tremendous sigh.

"Hanged?" Millicent asked.

"There was a spangle beneath his feet," Mehitabel whispered. "So you see."

"General Cuernos is dead?" Millicent demanded, more fearful for Anton than ever.

"He passed on violently," Missus Dovecote corrected her gently.

"They found him only a few minutes after it happened. The Emmorys heard a noise and called one of the stewards. When they found the door was locked, it was forced on the Captain's orders. The General was hanging from a bracket in the ceiling, with his hands tied behind his back." Mehitabel spoke compulsively, hardly stopping to breathe. "He hadn't been dead more than ten or fifteen minutes. The room was locked, and they say that there were strange markings on the walls of his cabin. And he was found with another spangle. There was no sign of a struggle."

"It is very distressing," Missus Dovecote intoned.

"Well, if you're thinking that Anton did it, he didn't. I've been down in the hold talking to him while he worked on his equipment." Millicent brought her chin up; she could tell from the expressions on the two women's faces that they did not believe her.

14

Captain Symington looked over the somber-faced diners and cleared his throat once more. "I truly regret the necessity of this decision, and you must believe that I do it with the utmost reluctance. If it were not for the calamities we have suffered, I would not instigate these measures, but the circumstances, you must all understand, force me to act."

"Commendable," one of the Scandinavian travelers said loudly enough to have the word carry through the entire room.

"As of this evening, we must ask all of you to remain in your quarters or, if you must venture out, to do so in the company of one of the members of the crew. We are also requesting that those who are traveling alone make an extra effort to protect themselves. The two who have been murdered were traveling alone, and this convinces me that it is necessary to be especially cautious in these instances."

There was a smattering of applause before the Captain went on.

"I must also warn you about the spreading of malicious and irresponsible rumors, which are at the very least unfounded supposition. If there were any one person who appeared to be responsible for these heinous crimes, that person would be confined and under guard at once. Those of you who look to find a villain without the most careful investigation and convincing proof are hindering, not aiding, our efforts to apprehend the man." He tapped his water glass with his fork. "Now, if you will all rise for a moment of silence in respect to those who have suffered because of this monster . . ."

There was a scrape and shuffling rustle as the first-class diners rose and bowed their heads. Then Captain Symington coughed and the meal was under way.

"I'm really not very hungry," Millicent said when the main course was brought. "Do you think I could have a little omelette or something of that sort?"

"It's beef Wellington, Miss Cathcart," the waiter said, tempting her.

"Yes, I can see that, and it looks delicious," Millicent said, as she had been trained to do. "But I wouldn't do it justice. Thank you."

"You really ought to eat something, my dear," Mehitabel said softly. "At a time like this, you have to keep up your strength. You don't know what tomorrow may bring."

At the next table, Anton sat quite by himself. The food on his plate had hardly been touched.

Impulsively Millicent turned in her chair to face him. "Would you like to join us, Anton?"

"Millicent!" hissed Mehitabel, plucking at her sleeve.

"It would be nice to have you eat with us," Millicent went on, paying no attention to her aunt.

Anton's smile was not a success. "Thank you. I doubt it would be wise."

"Please," Millicent said, adding, "I hate to see you look so sad."

"And you, Missus Reyns?" Anton asked Mehitabel. "How do you feel about my company?"

Mehitabel was thoroughly flustered. "If my niece has asked for your company, it is fitting for me to welcome you," she said, as was proper, though she glanced around the room nervously as she said it.

"Well, perhaps it would be less awkward if Millicent were to come and sit with me." Anton made the suggestion with a twitch at the corner of his mouth.

"I'd like that," Millicent said, rising before Mehitabel could object. "Yes, that's fine. You can be comfortable, Aunt, and I can talk with Anton." She picked up her napkin and moved to Anton's table, drawing up the chair before Anton could rise and hold it for her.

"This is most unwise, Millicent," Mehitabel whispered to her through her teeth. "Everyone will notice."

"Good," said Millicent serenely as she sat down across from Anton. "You look upset."

"I am upset," he said with candor. "I was a pariah when I was younger, and now it seems that I am to be one again."

"Well, that's no reason not to eat," Millicent pointed

out, indicating his plate. "You might as well enjoy your dinner."

"You and my governess would have got on very well," Anton said, trying to be severe and unable to repress a hint of a smile.

"Would we? I doubt it." Millicent studied his face with deep attention. "I ought to talk to you some more," she told him, "but not now."

"About what—another illusion?" He was trying to keep his tone light, but was not very successful.

"In a way. I want to find out why someone is trying to make it appear that you're a murderer." This bald statement—which took every ounce of courage she possessed—brought his head up as sharply as a slap would.

"What?" he demanded, his voice soft.

"I want to find out who is trying to make it appear that you're doing the killings. That's what's going on, isn't it?" She said this as demurely as she could, but there was excitement in her eyes.

"Millicent," Anton said, now a bit recovered from her announcement. "You humble me, you really do, but I can't let you get involved. You're probably right about your suspicions, but I haven't any idea why, and that means that there's danger around me, very real danger, and I won't have you risking so much for me."

"Then it's just as well that I don't need your permission." She was beginning to enjoy herself now, and as she spoke, she grew more confident. "I want to find out who this person is, and make him stop it."

"Don't," he said, very serious now. "I appreciate this more than you know, but I won't permit you to—"

"The thing is," she went on as if she were not interrupting him, "this is just like one of your magic tricks, with everyone's attention being focused in the wrong place. You taught me that, and it's time I used that lesson. There are too many questions that haven't been answered, and no one knows how to sift through them to get the right ones." She gave him a small, triumphant smile. "You see, I've been thinking about it."

Anton gave a resigned sigh. "And what have you decided?"

"First," she said, leaning forward and speaking with enthusiasm, though she continued to keep her voice low, "I decided that if you really wanted to kill someone, you'd do it less obviously. The way people have been dying, in locked rooms with spangles on the floor, it's as if there's a big sign saying *this way to guilty magician* over the bodies. That means to me that you couldn't have done it."

"I might be very clever," Anton suggested, entering into the spirit of her speculations. "I might make it appear that I did it in so obvious a way that it would make it seem impossible that I would be so foolish."

Millicent shook her head. "That would be too complicated and too risky, you know. It could backfire. You've shown me that the best illusions are very simple, so this is not a good argument. All right, that means someone is trying to make it appear that you are the one responsible, and once I can determine why, then it ought to be obvious who. It's like the 'Princess and the Flame,' or whatever you call it. Once you realize that the dress is part of the illusion, the rest falls into place quickly." Her eyes were very bright. "No one pays any notice to me. I can find out all sorts of things without being obvious."

"It's not a game, Millicent," he warned her with troubled eyes meeting hers. "Or if it is a game, it's deadly serious. Never forget that, Millicent."

"I know that already," she said, feeling a little exasperated. "I do remember what happened to General Cuernos and Mister Wingham, and those understewards. I don't want anything like that to happen to me."

"Nor do I," Anton said somberly. "I should forbid you to do anything on my behalf. I ought to tell your aunt to keep you from acting."

"But you won't, will you?" Millicent said, the beginnings of a real smile in her eyes.

"No," he admitted with a sigh. "I won't do that. I need all the help I can get. And I have a strong suspicion that if I told you not to, you'd go ahead anyway, and then no one would know for sure what you were up to, and you'd be running a greater risk than you already are." He nodded slowly. "You do remind me of myself."

Millicent decided to take this as a compliment. "I like to keep my mind clear and my eyes open. And you'd better eat your dinner."

"You're determined to do this, aren't you?" He dutifully picked up a few peas on his fork.

"Of course. I don't want to wait around, doing nothing, until something worse happens." She gave a very exaggerated yawn. "I couldn't bear it, you know, waiting around in my cabin forever, and to do nothing but read and eat isn't possible. So boring."

"You're a scamp, Millicent. The day is going to come when you're going to be formidable." He watched her as she went on.

"So don't worry. No matter what happens, I know you

didn't do it, and I'm going to make sure everyone else knows it, too. Sabina said that she lost some spangles off her costume, and I want to know when it happened."

"During the 'Princess and the Flame,' " Anton said. "When she got out of the costume."

"Oh." This took Millicent aback, but she recovered. Now that she had committed herself to investigate, the enormity of the task rushed in on her, and she doubted she was capable of doing so much. Yet she had promised, and she would not go back on her word.

"I'm very grateful, Millicent." Anton had taken a few more bites of his food and he seemed to be less downcast than before.

"Wait until I've done something," she said, hoping that she would not fail.

The next morning, Millicent appeared for breakfast early, and she was carrying a notebook and pen. "I'm trying to establish where everyone was when the murders took place," she explained to the nine passengers who were waiting to be served.

One of the French gentlemen laughed and remarked that it was good to find someone who thought their predicament was amusing.

"I'm not amused," Millicent said very seriously. "I'm very concerned for everyone's safety, and if we begin by learning where everyone was, then we'll have a place to begin."

"You're a most precocious youngster," one of the elderly Englishmen pronounced, giving Millicent an intimidating stare.

Missus Dovecote shuddered and said, "I dread to think

what your aunt must be feeling, Millicent. You've no consideration for her. You can't understand what your interference means to her."

"She already told me that it isn't proper for me to do this, and I said that propriety didn't matter when lives are at stake." Millicent folded her arms. "If each of you will give me a few minutes, I can make a note of where you were at the approximate times of the murders."

"Why not indulge her? If the Captain doesn't want her doing this, he'll soon put a stop to it." The French gentleman shrugged with aplomb. "Where's the harm in it, after all?"

There were a few grumbles, but most of the passengers were reluctantly willing to answer the questions Millicent had prepared. In less than an hour, she had spoken to more than fifteen of the passengers and was feeling that her venture might be a success in spite of everything.

At noon, with more than fifty sets of answers scribbled in her notebook, Millicent went down into the hold where Anton's show was stored.

Sabina was sewing up a rip in the costume she had worn while in the Iron Maiden, and she sneered at Millicent as she caught sight of her. "The Duke's not here," she said.

"I know; he's in his cabin with one of the stewards," Millicent said in her self-possessed way. "I was hoping Jibben would be able to talk with me."

"He's around here somewhere," Sabina said, her pretty face showing harsh lines from early poverty. "Not that he'll talk to you. He's the master's dog, and no doubt about it." She set her last two stitches savagely so that the thread almost broke.

"Would you tell me where I could find him?" Millicent asked as politely as she knew how.

"Why should I?" demanded Sabina, then she shook her head. "He'll find you if you stay here awhile." She stepped back to examine the costume. "It'll hold for a few more shows, I daresay."

"Doesn't it worry you, to have those long sharp spikes come so close to you?" Millicent asked, hoping that she might divert some of Sabina's attention from her other complaints.

"Not really; I know how it works, of course. If you didn't know what to do, you'd be punctured for sure. That's why the Duke always has someone inspect the inside, to make sure all the spikes are real. That they are. That they are." She relished this statement, and watched Millicent to find out how she felt about it.

"If the spikes are all genuine," Millicent said carefully, "then it is more your trick than Anton's, isn't it?"

"Too right," agreed Sabina, regarding Millicent with less suspicion than before. "You're as clever as can hold together, like the Duke says."

Jibben appeared from behind the Spirit Cabinet, his work clothes rumpled. "What are you doing here?"

"Fixing my costume," Sabina told him. "Some spangles came loose."

"Not you: her." His long, big-knuckled finger pointed at Millicent in a manner that was unfriendly.

"I need to talk to you," Millicent said, wishing her voice sounded less frightened.

"Talk away," he said. "But I won't say I'll answer." He folded his arms and sat down on the rough bench where he did small repairs.

"If you're going into discussions, I'm off. I've got a gentleman who wants to walk me around the deck. A very attractive man, tall and reserved. A bit skinny, too, but you can't have everything." She tossed her head and flounced out of the room.

Jibben made a rude gesture at her departing back. "She's come a long way from Whitechapel, but not as far as she thinks," he said.

"Has she been with Anton's show long?" Millicent inquired.

"Yes; she was with him in London, before he came to America. That was almost four years ago. We've been in America for three years, touring." He gave Millicent a measured look. "She wasn't much older than you are, back then. She'd been working in music halls for three years before that. I'll say this for her—she isn't afraid of hard work."

"Is working with Anton hard?" Millicent asked.

"Lord, yes. And she does her job well. I don't know who Anton will find to replace her once she hooks herself a husband." He fell silent. "What do you want to ask me?"

Millicent blinked, finding his abrupt manner disquieting. "I . . . I'd like to know what you were doing when the murders took place?"

"Nothing that matters to you or to Anton," Jibben answered.

"Oh," Millicent said, hoping he would volunteer some more.

"Is that all you intend to find out?" Jibben's question was once again abrupt.

"I thought I'd begin by finding out where everyone

was, and then try to determine what the victims might have in common.'' She said this in a rush, as if that would kindle a response in the English Gypsy.

''They're on the *Duchess of Malfi*, that's what they have in common,'' Jibben said, dismissing the whole thing. ''I warned him that it would happen again, and it has.''

''You warned him *what* would happen again?'' Millicent said, her breath catching in her throat with excitement.

''The attempts on his life, of course,'' Jibben said. ''Or hasn't he bothered to mention that?''

''There have been attempts on Anton's life before now?'' Millicent asked with ill-concealed amazement.

''Not Anton's: the Archduke's. You do know about that, don't you?'' Jibben sounded faintly contemptuous as he asked, as if everyone must be aware of Anton's past.

''Yes. He told me about it.'' She opened her notebook and found a clean page. ''Tell me about it, will you? And do you mind if I make notes?''

''Go ahead,'' he said to her.

15

"It was in the winter," Jibben said while Millicent struggled to keep up with him in her notebook. "We'd been in London about two years, a bit less, perhaps. There'd been an invitation to Anton to attend some sort of reception at the Austrian embassy, something to do with commemoration of the Emperor's rule, or marriage, or some anniversary or other. He didn't want to go. He tried to refuse gracefully, but one of His Majesty's functionaries came to see him and said that it would be appreciated if he would do this. After some discussion, Anton agreed." He glanced at Millicent. "Have you got all this?"

"Almost all," said Millicent honestly. "I might have to fill in later. Go on, please."

"As you wish." Jibben pulled a dark and vile-smelling pipe out of his pocket, and a pouch of tobacco from another pocket, and began to fill the pipe. "Well, the long and the short of it was that he went, and had to wear all the regalia. He kept saying that since he'd abdicated, there was no reason for it, but apparently the ambassador insisted, so there was nothing to be done. They sent him the ribbons and sashes and knee breeches so that he'd be correct. He belongs to one of those knightly orders that they have in Austria and Gemany and those places. He said the whole thing was archaic. You should have heard him carry on."

"Then the troupe knew about his past?" asked Millicent.

"Most of 'em, yes. A few didn't find out until that episode." He put the pipe between his teeth and struck a match. He drew a few times on the pipe and, satisfied that it was properly lit, went on. "He went to the reception and the rest of it, and came back late at night, sizzling with outrage and reeking of cognac. It seems that someone there had approached him privately about a plan to establish Bohemia as a separate country, and they wanted him to join with them in their plot. Anton's the wrong man to enlist in a scheme of that kind." He chuckled. "He fumed for three days, and everyone in the troupe went around on tiptoe for fear of setting him off again."

"That wasn't the end of it, was it?" Millicent asked, knowing the answer already.

"No, it wasn't," said Jibben more thoughtfully. "It was more the beginning." He took his pipe from between his teeth and pointed it at her. "I had better not be making a mistake in telling you all this, but since Anton trusts you, I'll give you the benefit of the doubt: remember that."

"I will," Millicent promised.

"Good. I'll hold you to that," he said calmly, which gave his words more impact. "And in the meantime, consider what I tell you. It was less than a week later during a show when he was doing the bullet catch—"

"The one where he catches the bullet in his teeth, as he did here?" Millicent clarified.

"That one, yes. Someone in the audience stood up and fired a gun at him, calling out that he should catch this bullet, too, or similar words. He carries the scar on his neck and shoulder and will bear it to the end of his life. It was lucky that the man was a poor shot; he would have killed Anton had he been better."

Millicent felt her spine go cold. "They *shot* him? Really?"

"Yes," Jibben said, taking his pipe between his teeth.

"Who was the man?" Millicent asked.

"A seaman, off a German ship. He told the police he thought that magicians could always do that sort of thing." He sighed. "Anton filed charges, but the matter never came to trial."

"Why not?" Millicent wanted to know, feeling more indignation than fright.

"Because the German Government requested that the man be sent back to Germany for any trial. There were diplomatic strings pulled and the fellow disappeared. That was the end of the matter for a while."

"You mean there's more?" Millicent asked, aghast.

"At first there were a few minor accidents, things that might be nothing more than mischance. They happened over a period of three months, after Anton returned to the show. Then there were other troubles. Anton's carriage was pursued one night by some hooligans who were throwing rocks and bottles and, as it turned out, knives. He wasn't hurt, but that was merely his good fortune. He had a fire in his dressing room and a box of poisoned sweets left for him at the stage door. In fact, one of the reasons he accepted the American tour was to get away. He said that if he took time for the others to cool off, he could perform again without risking his life and the lives of his troupe." He cleared his throat. "I warned him that once they begin, they don't stop until the job is done. Now that he is on his way back to Europe, I fear that Anton is once more a target."

"But why not kill him? Why go to the trouble of killing other people?" Millicent frowned and looked up from the page. "That's what has me troubled, Jibben. Why should they bother? And who are they?"

"They will do this to be rid of Anton—Tancred—so that he is not a rallying point. A murdered archduke is a martyr, no matter who killed him or why. An abdicated archduke who is a murderer is nothing more than an embarrassment, best forgotten." Jibben bit down on the stem of his pipe and regarded Millicent closely. "I don't know who they are, and if Anton knows, he has not told me. If the deaths continue, they will follow him no matter what, because he was here, because there were rumors. You see what that will do. It will mean," he went on, answering his own question, "that there is no possibility of returning him to his duchy."

"But he doesn't want to return to his duchy," said Millicent at her most reasonable. "He told me so himself."

"You and I are convinced of this, because we know him. The men who seek to discredit him do not believe it because they cannot conceive that anyone would willingly sacrifice this opportunity." His face looked older, as if he had suddenly grown very tired. "I have talked to him of this, but he hasn't given it much credence. Now it may be too late."

"Because of the murders and the suspicions," Millicent said, following Jibben's train of thought.

"Once this ship docks, the rumors will fly, no matter what is finally learned or who is caught." His humor darkened more.

"Then we must apprehend the real murderer before then," said Millicent with great purpose. "That's why I'm getting all these notes, although I've yet to make sense of them." She did not allow herself to be disheartened, for although the work ahead seemed overwhelming, she knew that to hesitate now was disaster.

"And what have you discovered?" Jibben asked her, his tone little more than polite.

"That there are no apparent connections from one victim to the next, and for that matter, no apparent connections to Anton." She let herself sigh. "There must be something. I know I'm missing something."

"Not to Anton, not to each other?" Jibben repeated.

"Not that I can find," she confessed. "And any other connections haven't become obvious yet. I thought it might be financial, but Mister Wingham didn't have much money, according to rumor, and the understeward had none, so that isn't the reason."

"You must persevere," he said, not with a great deal of confidence. "Something will suggest itself."

"Yes, you're right," she said, getting up from the other end of the bench. "And it's time I went to ask more questions. Most of the passengers cooperate because they think it's amusing that I should bother with the case at all. One of them called me plucky." It irritated her to admit this, as it seemed to cast doubt on her abilities.

"Do not be troubled if you cannot learn everything. There isn't much time, and resources are limited aboard a ship," Jibben said, and drew on his foul-smelling pipe.

"How can you say that?" Millicent demanded. "I will be mortified if I don't succeed, and Anton, as you've already explained, will have to live with the results of my failure, not I."

"True enough," said Jibben slowly.

"Don't doubt the importance of what I'm doing," she said with great force. "I know I'm only fourteen, but no one else is doing anything. I know that there are responsibilities in these killings, and I want to find out who and what is behind them."

"I encourage you, don't misunderstand," said Jibben, becoming impatient. "My only reservation is for your safety. You're taking great risks. I know something of the kind of men who play these deadly games, and they will not hesitate to do away with you if they find you are making real progress."

"I'll remember that," said Millicent, closing her notebook and preparing to leave. "Thank you for what you've told me. It doesn't help much yet, but it gives me a new direction to pursue."

"Good," Jibben said. He waved his hand to dismiss her.

"I will keep you informed." She was already halfway to the door.

"I'd appreciate that." He shook his head slowly. "And take care, girl."

Millicent beamed at him, hating to tell him how much she was enjoying herself. She hurried away, her mind so active that she almost ran into Missus Dovecote, who was taking the air on the deck, pushing her husband's wheeled chair before her, in a rare moment of wifely care.

"Your aunt has been looking for you," Missus Dovecote said to Millicent, making the words an accusation.

"I've been busy," Millicent said, trying to placate Missus Dovecote with half a curtsy.

"It's all very well for you to say that, young lady, but it doesn't calm Mehitabel's nerves, which are sadly shattered." She was determined to impress Millicent with her failings, for she went on fervently, "Your aunt is a dear, good soul who has suffered much. Youth is very thoughtless of the travail of others, and you are no exception. It behooves you to show more consideration to Mehitabel; it is your duty to do so."

"I will," Millicent said, thinking that she wanted to tell Missus Dovecote that if Mehitabel was put out with her, it was her aunt's place to say so, not Missus Dovecote's.

"You're very headstrong, Millicent. It isn't becoming," said Missus Dovecote as a parting shot.

Millicent shrugged and continued on to her cabin, hoping she would have the chance to go over all her notes before evening.

By late afternoon, it was apparent that nearly all the passengers in first class had decided that Anton had something to do with the murders, and made a point of avoiding him. This was made more emphatic when one of the British passengers overheard the chief steward, Vaclav Roman, tell the other stewards that, the night before, he had seen a body floating in the air over the fantail, and he was certain that it presaged another death.

"I knew we were not over the ordeal," Missus Dovecote said to Mehitabel as they sat in Mehitabel and Millicent's cabin. "I am so downcast that I can hardly bear to speak of it." With this announcement, she plunged into her impressions. "It was one thing when the crewman was washed overboard, although now I am not at all certain that he was not a victim like the others. Now that the passengers are being killed, and in such bizarre manners, it fills me with the keenest dread that we will all be caught by this raving lunatic."

"We ought to have another sitting," Mehitabel said vaguely. "Perhaps your spirit guides can shed some light on—"

"I could not think of it," interrupted Auralia Dovecote. "I could not endure to be the bearer of ill tidings, which is what I fear I must be. Certainly, if there are any more murders, I will feel it incumbent upon me to act and use my poor talents to do what I can to apprehend the criminal, but now it is too much to ask." She put her hand to her bosom and gazed forlornly at the porthole. "Who would have thought that such terrible events would overtake us on what promised to be so pleasant a journey?"

"Please, Auralia," said Mehitabel. "Don't distress yourself. It's bad enough to have all these unexplained deaths . . ." She got up from the sofa and went to the sideboard. "We must support the Captain's actions, and try to remain as calm as possible."

"For one who has been touched by these calamities, it is truly wonderful that you are able to be so collected," said Auralia Dovecote, adding with a swift and irritated glance toward the chair where Millicent sat poring over what she had written in her notebook, "And I am sure it is not because you have been given much help."

"Now, then, Auralia," said Mehitabel, unexpectedly upholding her niece, "I cannot condemn Millicent for her efforts to get to the bottom of these mysteries. I wish that more of our traveling companions were as constructively inclined."

"Just so," said Missus Dovecote with one of her abrupt changes of mental direction. "It does you much credit, this encouragement of Millicent in the midst of trouble."

Millicent refused to be drawn into the debate between the women, and she thought that both Missus Dovecote and her aunt were being melodramatic. She continued to condense her notes.

"Millicent is very studious," Mehitabel said, sounding more troubled than proud. "It is just as well to allow her an opportunity to—"

"No doubt," cut in Missus Dovecote. "In the meantime, you and I are left without consolation. Well, that is ever the way of the world." She stood up. "Take a turn about the deck with me, won't you, Mehitabel? That way your scholar can be left to her studies, and we will be obeying the Captain's strictures that everything be done in the company of others."

"And what of Millicent? She'll be quite alone." It was obvious that Mehitabel was longing for the chance to get out, but could not bring herself to desert her niece.

"Oh, no one is going to be suspicious of a child," said Auralia with a wave of her hand. "All we need do is tell the chief steward that she is in the cabin, and they will send one of the stewards to watch the hallway." She was already gathering up her boa and slinging it around her shoulders.

Mehitabel allowed herself to be persuaded. "You're right, I trust. And it would be marvelous to get out." She looked thoughtfully at Millicent. "Would you mind?"

"It's a very good idea, Aunt Mehitabel," said Millicent, doing her best not to sound relieved. "So long as one of the stewards is told where I am, there should be no question. You need to take time to enjoy yourself."

"As if that's possible," lamented Missus Dovecote even while she held the door open for Mehitabel to leave the cabin.

"Be sure to lock the door as soon as we're gone. I'll rap twice when we return." Mehitabel was securing her large hat to her head with a gauze scarf.

"Locked doors have not stopped the murderer," murmured Missus Dovecote as she and Mehitabel left Millicent alone with her notes.

In the Grand Salon that night, everyone was very quiet, and many were decidedly nervous. One of the British passengers tended to laugh too loudly and too often, and one of the Frenchmen was openly hostile to those around him. Instead of the friendly banter that had marked this gathering on previous evenings, there was almost no conversation, and what there was tended to be confined to short bursts and terse replies.

"The Captain has asked me to announce," said the chief steward when all of the first-class passengers had gathered, "that a policy of nightlong patrols of all the companionways—hallways and staircases—will begin tonight. You will all be locked into your cabins and a strict curfew of ten o'clock will be observed. We apologize in advance for the inconvenience, but I assure you it is quite necessary."

"Why not simply lock up that magician fellow?" demanded one of the German passengers.

Anton, standing at the rear of the room, straightened but did nothing to remind the passengers of his presence.

"Fat lot of good that would do," countered one of the Englishmen. "He'd simply get out and kill someone for the sport of it. Leave one of those blasted spangle things to taunt us."

"Yes, the way he got out of those chains," Missus Dovecote said to Mehitabel in an undervoice.

"That was just a trick," Millicent said scornfully.

"If we're locked up," objected Jared Emmory, "might it not make us all more of a target rather than less?" He heard the affirmative reaction from others around him. "I think the patrol is an excellent notion, but to be confined with no means of escape, and in the presence of a killer who laughs at locks, well, it seems to be more of a chance than I'd like to take."

"Very good, Mister Emmory," said Miss Gordon. "And for those of us traveling alone, the risk is much greater, for it appears that the killer—whoever it may be—selects victims at random from those who are by themselves."

"I believe that the patrol is necessary," said Milton Homes in his whispery voice from the place where he huddled in the corner. "It is most important that we all be protected. As another passenger traveling alone, I feel most vulnerable. I fear that many more nights like the last few and I will succumb to a nerve storm. I'm overwrought as it is."

"Amen to that," said an elderly American lady who held a vial of smelling salts in one gloved hand.

"The patrol is a very good notion," said the youngest of the Frenchmen. "As to the locks, those who wish can agree; the rest will have to discuss the matter with the Captain."

This plan gained the greatest support, and by the time the passengers went in to dinner, Chief Steward Roman had started to work out the schedules for the nightlong patrol.

"While this is being arranged," said Anton as he took his place in the dining room, "I want it understood that my door is to be locked from the outside, and the lock inspected every hour."

"Not that it means anything with such a person," muttered one of the Americans.

Millicent sighed as she sat down beside Mehitabel.

16

"It's the second navigator," the understeward exclaimed as he came running down the narrow hall.

Three of the early risers saw him, and one asked the man to stop. "What about the second navigator?"

"I must tell the Captain," said the understeward, breaking away from the three men.

"Did you see his face?" asked Milton Homes of the others, his voice quavering. "He was white."

"Not another murder!" a straight-backed German professor said, his tone harsh with disgust.

"I trust not," said the third man, his hands joined behind his back and his manner pompous.

"What if it is?" quavered Milton Homes. "I tell you, I'm terrified."

The third man made a gesture of distaste and the German professor said, "You're jumping to conclusions, sir.

It is hardly conclusive that because one of the stewards is upset, it must be that there has been another killing."

"You're right," Mister Homes said, chastened, "but I can't help worrying."

"Who of us can?" asked the third man with a lift of his head that showed he was not the least afraid himself and thought less of men who were.

"We'll find out what happened by breakfast. In the meantime," said the German professor, "I have still three more circuits of the deck to complete before they start serving us."

Milton Homes hung back. "I . . . don't think I can face food just now, if you'll excuse me . . ." He turned away, running along the deck, his thin frame more hunched over than usual.

By the time breakfast was over, it was learned that the second navigator had been found stabbed to death in his cabin, the door securely locked and the man appearing to have died without a struggle.

"Oh, dear, if there were somewhere we could *go,*" cried Mehitabel as she and Millicent left the dining room. "To be forever in the cabin, strolling the deck, or eating is the most nerve-racking thing imaginable." She was wearing a subdued, high-waisted suit of navy blue twill, and her very wide hat with the pheasant feathers, which was more appropriate to an autumn shopping expedition than to the *Duchess of Malfi.* "I must speak with Auralia. This is simply hideous."

Millicent listened dutifully, but her mind was occupied with the notes she had made. How could the second navigator be connected with Mister Wingham and General

Cuernos? There might be some link to the understeward, but the rest baffled her. She frowned as the questions grew more perplexing.

"Auralia must consent to another sitting now that this has happened. With her gift, she might be able to determine how the deeds were done. Another locked room!" Mehitabel walked faster in her agitation. "It is so ghastly. I knew how it would be from the first."

"You can't believe that," said Millicent testily. "And it doesn't help anyone to have you repeating this."

Mehitabel's expression was rigid with disapproval. "If you are so shocked by these events that you have wholly forgotten yourself, then it might be as well for you to go to the cabin for an hour or so, until you remember how to conduct yourself." The severity of this rebuke showed how deeply affected Mehitabel was.

"All right," said Millicent, turning away from her aunt at once.

"And I do not mean for you to go anywhere else, miss. I will not have you seeing that magician, who, for all we know, is the one who is committing these terrible crimes. He is not a proper person; men of his sort have no breeding, and they take advantage of those who are their betters. Keep that in mind." Mehitabel had raised her voice, and so attracted some attention.

"Quite right," agreed a well-dressed older man with a ginger moustache. "They give themselves airs if you let them."

Mehitabel was pleased for this support. "Thank you, sir. My niece, like many another girl before her, is more impressionable than she realizes."

"What do you know of it?" asked Millicent rudely as

she fled, feeling outraged and embarrassed, knowing that if her aunt had any notion of Anton's heritage, she would fawn on him as eagerly as she now condemned him. Millicent wanted to scream or stamp her feet at the unfairness, but she refused to be so childish.

The worst revelation came a little later, when one of the crewmen—it might have been the chief steward, no one was quite certain—let slip the information that, that morning, the locks on Anton's cabin door had been discovered broken on the outside. This new tidbit spread at once through all the first-class passengers and was improved in the telling, so that by the time Captain Symington called them all to a meeting in the Grand Ballroom, it was believed that the locks had disappeared entirely and that Anton himself had done the deed from inside his cabin, removing the locks and then passing out the door unheeded by clouding the minds of the crewmen on patrol so that they took no notice of him.

"And you know, they say that there was a spangle outside his door, as a reminder of what he had done," an excitable Dutch matron exclaimed just as Anton strolled into the Grand Ballroom.

His eyes were sunken and his face a bit pale from lack of sleep, and he looked around in ill-concealed irritation at the murmur of alarm that greeted his entrance.

Captain Symington was quick to address the matter. "That is what I wish to bring up," he said without preamble. "I wish to mention some of the irresponsible and superstitious rumors that have been hindering the investigations of my men and have distorted what few findings we have."

Anton took a seat some little distance from the others, keeping his attitude faintly aloof.

"I have been hearing gossip," Captain Symington went on with more firmness, "that borders on accusations. That is a very serious state of affairs. Some of you are saying or implying that the Incredible Anton has been party to the crimes aboard this vessel. Until such allegations are proven, anyone repeating those rumors is committing slander and will be treated accordingly. To begin with, you will be confined to your cabin and served by the stewards."

Anton spoke up. "Captain, in light of this, I would appreciate being put under armed guard, either in my quarters or through having an officer and crewman in my company at all times. It is inconvenient for everyone but might serve as a deterrent to some of the speculation that has been going on."

"If I think it necessary—" the Captain began and was interrupted by a number of shouts and objections.

"It doesn't matter what you do to him," one of the women shrieked. "He's a magician. He can pass through walls! He's done it on that stage."

"In that case," said Anton with great fatigue, "why would I bother to break the locks on my door? I understand that is supposed to have happened."

"Magicians have limits to their powers," called out Missus Dovecote with great authority. "In order to retain your power, you must have victims to offer to the devil. When you have not done so, then your powers wane until your sacrifice is complete."

"Oh, excellent, Auralia," seconded Mehitabel, gazing in awe at her new friend.

"Sacrifices? The devil?" Anton repeated incredulously. "I am a performer, madame. I do illusions. Nothing you see is happening as you think it is." He rubbed his forehead. "Captain, I beg you, make some provision for me. In a climate like this, the situation is too volatile."

"That may be premature," Captain Symington said firmly in an effort to bring order to the assembly.

"If there are any more incidents, it will certainly be too late," Anton interjected. "I am willing to have all my equipment locked up. My assistant has said she does not want to perform until the murderer is apprehended. She has good reason to feel as she does, and I will not force her. My associate has assured me that he can secure all my equipment in the hold and will make sure it is locked and guarded. Anything more that will put an end to this current assumption that I have had anything to do with the killings I will gladly do." He had risen and was facing the Captain. "I am asking for my own protection as well as yours."

"Charlatan!" called out one of the British travelers.

"Certainly," Anton responded. "So long as it brings everyone to their senses, I will be anything you like." He turned to the room. "I hope that all of you realize that this determination to fix the guilt on me allows the real criminal to act almost unimpeded. There is no reason for him to be cautious when he knows that you are all willing to believe that I am the murderer." He opened his hands in a gesture of appeal. "Please, keep an open mind. All of you."

Millicent, who had been listening with aching sympathy, got up and, shaking off her aunt's restraining hand, walked over to where Anton stood. "I'm not afraid to be

Anton's friend," she said, her voice quivering a bit as she saw the concentrated disapproval of the other passengers.

"You're a foolish and headstrong child," said Missus Dovecote, "and a shame to your aunt."

Miss Gordon spoke up. "Everything Anton has said makes good sense. We have permitted ourselves to be led into a very blind state of mind. Anton is an easy target because of what he does. Most of us have enjoyed watching him work his wonders for us, and that has persuaded us that he is more than a performer. It would be more to our credit if we were to take his part and give him the benefit of the doubt we would give any other passenger aboard." Her stern good sense had a dampening effect on the humor of the gathering.

"She's right," one of the other passengers said grudgingly.

Mister Emmory rose. "For the time being, I think it would be wise to continue the patrols, and to insist that one of the passengers accompany the members of the crew, so that there is an opportunity for us to act rather than to sit waiting for developments. I volunteer to accompany any of the patrols that you, Captain, assign me to."

Captain Symington looked over the first-class passengers. "I am pleased that you are starting to be sensible. I am fully cognizant of the terrible deeds that have taken place, and anyone with sensibility cannot be untouched by these dreadful events. However, it is not in the interests of anyone aboard to find a scapegoat, no matter how convenient. I will post the passenger additions to the patrols in the Grand Salon within the hour, and I request that anyone hearing any rumors whatever do his utmost to stifle those rumors at once."

"You shouldn't have done this," Anton said softly to Millicent as the meeting came to an end.

"Someone had to," she said reasonably, trying to forget the wrenching fear that had seized her as she saw the hostility in the eyes of the others. Their disapproval stung her more than she wanted to admit, even to herself.

"It ought not to have been you," he said, "but I thank you for doing it. Your aunt will probably want to hang me from the yardarm, or whatever they do on ocean liners." He was trying to lighten their mood, but did not succeed.

"Anton," Millicent asked seriously, "why don't you tell the Captain about who you are and the other times . . ." She stopped, unable to find a way to express herself.

"What other times?" Anton asked carefully. He was watching the passengers as they started to leave the Grand Ballroom. None of them approached him or offered any indication of apology for their behavior.

"In London, when you were shot," she said flatly, looking up at him as the harsh lines deepened in his face.

"And how did you learn about that, pray?" he asked sweetly.

"I've talked to Jibben, and he told me. I was trying to find some association between the victims, and Jibben agreed to answer my questions. Don't be angry with him, Anton. He did it for your good. He didn't want to tell me." She could see how set his face was, and how bright his eyes had become.

"I see. He will have to explain it to me," Anton said.

"There's nothing to explain," Millicent told him. "He is as concerned for you as I am—probably more—and if that's not sufficient explanation, then I do not know what would be."

Some of the severity of Anton's demeanor faded. "You're right, of course, little as I like to admit it." He sat down slowly. "Very well, tell me what you have been up to. I'll try to listen, but I warn you that I'm not in a very amiable frame of mind just now."

"That's hardly surprising," said Millicent, sitting in the chair beside him. "And with everything you've been through, it's probably worse than I think." She took her notebook out of her small kid purse. "I haven't been able to find anything that ties the victims together, but I think that it might be wise for you to talk to the Captain. He's a reasonable man, isn't he? He might have some idea of the best way to handle everything."

"He's doing that already," Anton said darkly.

"But on inadequate information. If he knew who you used to be, then he might take a different view of things. If you told him about the previous attempts on your life, then he might be willing to see you're guarded, and if it is you they're after, you won't have to be so exposed." Millicent had been developing her arguments in her mind since breakfast, but now that she spoke them, they seemed insufficient to overcome Anton's reticence.

"Millicent, I appreciate your efforts, and I'm deeply in your debt. But you must let me do this as I think best." He started to rise as Mehitabel approached, bristling with indignation. "Your aunt needs you, Millicent."

"No she doesn't," Millicent said, but rose with him.

"Young lady," Mehitabel said as she came up to the

two, "your behavior is disgraceful. I am shocked and distressed at what you've done, and I will so inform your father when I write to him about this voyage, which you may be certain I will do." She rounded on Anton. "As to you, sir, you are the most loathsome parvenu to set foot on this ship, and if you continue to abuse the confidence of my niece, I will have a great deal to say about it."

"You already have, Missus Reyns," said Anton with only a trace of sarcasm. "As to your niece, her willingness to support a friend in trouble is more heroic than gauche. Or so I've always been taught." With that, he inclined his head to Mehitabel and turned toward the Captain.

"What effrontery!" Mehitabel blustered as she took Millicent firmly by the wrist. "I think that a morning spent on your studies is in order, miss. And I want to hear no more about this unseemly association with that Anton person. If your father knew that you were befriending a performer, he would be disgusted."

Millicent followed her aunt to the door, reflecting that if her father knew she had befriended an archduke, he would be delighted.

17

"The main trouble is that the rooms were locked, that's what it seems to be," said Millicent as she read from her notebook. At her elbow, Jibben barked with laughter.

"Girl, there's no trick to that—it is an easy matter to rig these doors to lock upon closing, and not so much more difficult to get a pass key from one of the crewmen." He looked toward the bow of the *Duchess of Malfi,* his eyes narrowed. "You find out how the murderer got into the rooms, and why, and I will show you how he got out." He rose from the bench and indicated the second-class deck. "The passengers here have been untouched. No one has paid much attention, except to be amused that those in first class should be killed for their privileges."

Millicent tried to conceal her discouragement. "I ought to start over, I guess."

"Not start over," said Jibben. "You have much good information, and now you have only to sift the wheat from the chaff. Anton tells me that you deduced most of how the 'Princess and the Flame' is done; this should not be any more difficult for you." He started away fom her and then said, "Talk to me again soon. Between us, there may still be a solution."

"I will," she said, feeling overwhelmed. She gathered up her purse and her notebook and returned to the first-class levels of the liner, sunk deeply in study. She was so distracted by her thoughts that she very nearly did not notice Miss Gordon, who sat alone in a deck chair.

"Miss Cathcart," Miss Gordon repeated. "Millicent. Would you mind my talking with you?" This was so tenuously said that Millicent was startled into attention.

"Of course; what is it?" She took the deck chair next to Miss Gordon's and sat down, closing her notebook and tucking it into the pocket of her coat. "Is something the matter?"

"You ask that, after what has happened?" Miss Gordon asked in strained tones.

"I'm sorry," Millicent apologized at once, realizing that Miss Gordon was not only upset, she was frightened. "If there's anything I can do?"

"I don't know that you can," said Miss Gordon, doing her best to regain her composure. "But you're not as taken in as the others, and I gather you know how some of those magical tricks are done. I want to learn a little of that, if you'll bear with me."

"I don't know very much," Millicent cautioned. "Anton has let me guess a few things, that's all."

"But you can tell if something *is* an illusion, can't you?" Miss Gordon asked, her eyes becoming desperate.

Millicent was about to make a joking answer, and then

stopped the words in her throat. "I might be able to. And I can ask Anton."

"No!" protested Miss Gordon. "Don't do that, please. If I'd wanted him to know of this, I would have approached him myself. I want you to hear me out, not him." She fiddled with the frogging on her ankle-length coat. "I . . . I don't know quite where to begin."

"Anywhere you wish," Millicent said, thinking that Miss Gordon might need more time to order her questions. She filled in the silence by remarking that it was turning very chilly.

"Yes, it is," said Miss Gordon, a bit more briskly. "But that hardly matters." She clasped her hands together and struggled to relay what had happened. "It was last night, and I had not been in bed very long. I was reading in the hope that I would become sleepy, for I was nervous and restless. I was reading *The People of the Abyss,* by that California writer, and ordinarily the plight of those poor people would have . . ." Her words trailed off, and she shook herself sternly. "That is nothing to the point. The book did not hold my wonted attention and . . . I was soon . . . captivated by . . . what appeared to be a figure floating outside my porthole." She said the last as if she were confessing some guilty secret, such as an uncontrollable passion for the drink absinthe. "I thought that I was half asleep and dreaming—you know the dreams that seem real—and that nothing was happening at all. And then I looked around the room, trying to break the spell of it, and to determine whether I was truly awake or not." She fell abruptly silent once again.

"Were you awake?" asked Millicent when Miss Gordon did not continue.

"I am reasonably sure that I was, but . . . dreams are very convincing, aren't they?" She made an unconvincing laugh.

"Some of mine have been," said Millicent judiciously. "One or two remained with me, sharp as real memories." She wondered what it was that was bothering Miss Gordon that made her think of dreams.

"I decided that this was not one, but that doesn't mean it was not," said Miss Gordon, the doubt coming back into her face. "I saw in the far corner of the room, where the shadows were the deepest, the figure of a man, a tall, lean man, hanging there, looming over me." She put her hands over her mouth and refused to go on.

"Did you summon aid?" asked Millicent, becoming very curious.

"Yes, eventually, and there was nothing there. No other person was in my room, and my door was locked, but . . . I still think of that shadow, and I cannot persuade myself that there was nothing to it but my overactive imagination." This last was more argumentative, and Miss Gordon would not meet Millicent's eyes.

"Why did you think it was a real person?" Millicent inquired, doing her best to sound unruffled.

"Because of how it looked," Miss Gordon admitted. "There was a presence, almost a scent, an odor of a person in the air. When I mentioned it to the steward who answered my call, he told me that at sea there are many strange smells, and those who are not used to ships can be confused." Now there was pique in her manner. Millicent wondered what Miss Gordon had replied to the steward.

"He could be correct, or it may also be that the unfamiliar scents of the ocean and this ship might disguise other odors which you would notice at another time." In one of the detective tales she had read during her crossing to New York, Millicent recalled a villain who had used gas fumes to bring about hallucinations in order to throw the hero off his track.

"Why would anyone bother to do that?" Miss Gordon asked, very perplexed. "I am more troubled by that aspect than any other in the event," she said as if this were a shameful thing to tell anyone.

"I would be, as well," said Millicent, wanting to tell Miss Gordon all her suspicions, but hesitating. "You have been more . . . sensible than some of the others since the killings started. Maybe someone doesn't like that, and wants to change your attitude." She said it flippantly, but as soon as the words were out, they seemed very right to her.

"Much more of this, and I will change my attitude," Miss Gordon said, dejected again. "It's very daunting to realize that there can be such things in the world—events and pressures that strike at the very heart of your principles in this way."

Millicent thought of all she had learned about Anton and knew that he would understand Miss Gordon's dilemma better than anyone aboard. "If anything strange happens again, write down everything you notice, and that includes smells and tastes and sounds. It could be important. It might answer some of the questions." She hesitated, then continued. "You say you saw a figure: will you describe it for me?" She opened her notebook and brought her pen out of her purse.

Miss Gordon looked startled. "It was tall and lean, as

I've said. A man, perhaps as much as six feet in height, ramrod-straight, as they say, thin. His features weren't distinct, but I believe that the nose was pointed."

"Pointed how?" asked Millicent.

"How? Very straight and pointed." She watched Millicent scribble this down. "Is that important?"

"I don't know," said Millicent, candidly enough. "But I think that until I am sure that it isn't important, I'd better make a note of it." She thought of Anton's face with his impressive, beaky nose, and was secretly relieved. Whatever image Miss Gordon had seen was not Anton's.

"I've wanted to talk this over with someone. It was good of you to listen. Anyone else would assume that I had fallen prey to my fancies or was simply making a feminine bid for attention. I despise that behavior in women!" She shivered, partially from cold, partially from the strength of her emotions.

"You ought to tell the Captain. Just don't mention how frightened you were, and tell him that you don't put any stock in it. He'll hear you out." Millicent was proud of herself for being able to offer the competent Miss Cloris Gordon some useful advice.

"Yes; I should have done that before now," she agreed, very nearly recovered. "This is such a dreadful business. I assumed when I came on this voyage that I would have an opportunity to relax before beginning my studies. The worst I believed would happen to me was that I might be seasick."

"At least you have not been that," Millicent pointed out, trying to be amusing.

"True enough," said Miss Gordon seriously. "And yet I think I'd trade all these terrible killings for a continuous bout of seasickness. One recovers from seasickness." She folded her hands and regarded Millicent for a time. "You were very good to hear me out. And I must confess that your presence of mind puts me to the blush."

"I never saw a shadow in my cabin," Millicent reminded her. "If I did, I'd probably feel very differently."

Miss Gordon smiled her chagrin. "You're a very tactful young woman, and I admire you for it." She straightened the skirt of her coat, although it was not necessary.

"Talk with the Captain, Miss Gordon. It would be the wisest thing to do." Millicent closed her notebook and got up. "If you don't mind, I want to talk to Anton's assistant. There might be the tools for the kind of illusion you saw somewhere in his properties, and if there are, I think we should all know about it."

"Gracious, yes," said Miss Gordon. "A sterling notion. You are quite right." She got up from the deck chair. "And I will seek out the Captain. A little enterprise is all that's wanted." She started toward the doors, then said to Millicent, "In case I haven't made it apparent, your help has been most valuable."

"Thank you," said Millicent, already planning what she would say to Jibben.

The hold was dark, and Millicent entered it hesitantly. "Jibben?" she called. "I have another question or two." When there was no answer, she stepped through the door and made her way—as much by touch as sight—through the various magical equipment, taking care to upset nothing. "Jibben?"

There was a sound toward the back of the hold, and

behind the bulk of the Spirit Cabinet, Millicent could see a small light burning.

"Is that you, Jibben?" she called, but not very loudly. For some reason, she was filled with apprehension.

"Silence!" ordered a harsh voice from the other side of the Spirit Cabinet.

"I tell you, Helmut, no one's here," Sabina hissed.

"Keep your voice down! How do you know that disgusting Gypsy hasn't come back?"

"Because he's with Anton, that's why," Sabina answered saucily, but with a lowered voice.

"We must be cautious, in case he returns early," Helmut ordered Sabina.

Very carefully Millicent eased open the back of the Spirit Cabinet, glad that Jibben had oiled the hinges recently. As she listened, she climbed inside, looking for the front panels and hoping the crack between the doors would be wide enough for her to see who was talking to Sabina.

"All right," Sabina sulked.

"I'm getting tired of your delays, Sabina," Helmut—whoever that was—said after a brief pause.

"Too bad for you, ducks," snapped Sabina. "I'm not helping you again. I don't mind seeing a few of the nobs get theirs, but I'm not doing myself out of a job, neither."

"My dear, remember your aunt before you say that. What happened to her could very well befall you." Helmut's voice was smooth, and the threat was worse because of it.

"I—" Sabina began.

"Which was she, again? The one with her liver taken out, or did the Ripper merely slit her throat?" Helmut had a chuckle like a rake over pebbles. "Liz Stride. We only remember her because of who killed her. Ironic, isn't it?"

"Stop that," Sabina said, but now there was real fear in her tone.

Millicent pressed her face close to the crack in the Spirit Cabinet and peered out into the hold. She glimpsed Sabina's hair and part of a man's face, but not enough to recognize him.

"It is possible that the same fate could be yours. Admittedly, I haven't the reputation of Jack the Ripper, but I have more victims to my credit."

"It's easy enough to say," scoffed Sabina, but without any real confidence.

"And true." Helmut paused again. "The persons paying me expect to have Anton disposed of legally. I've accepted half their money and I intend to earn the other half. No one has ever been disappointed by Helmut Granz before, and I promise you, they will not be now; certainly not because a slum-born tart decides that she has a few theatrical engagements to protect."

There was something about Helmut's voice that was tantalizingly familiar. Millicent strained to hear more, to identify the speaker, but could not do so. She dared not move too much in the Spirit Cabinet for fear of opening it accidentally.

"Who are you calling a tart?" demanded Sabina, her voice raised in indignation. "You're the one who was paying court to me, all fancy words and posies, weren't you? If I'm a tart, what does that make you?"

Her defiance ended as he struck her. "Stop that!" Helmut ordered. "I will have no more of this. Either you will continue providing what I want, or you will meet with a fatal accident, one that will implicate your employer, naturally."

"Sodding beast!" Sabina whimpered.

"By all means," Helmut said nastily. "Now get me those lanterns."

"I won't," sobbed Sabina.

Millicent decided that she had to go for help. If she were to remain much longer, this Helmut might carry through his threat and kill Anton's pretty assistant. She inched her way back in the Spirit Cabinet, feeling for the one uneven plank that would release the back panel that Anton had shown her. Her heart was thudding, loud as an automobile engine in her ears, and she opened her mouth wide to breathe so that she would not be heard panting.

"Yes, jade, you will," Helmut said, his harsh voice alive with menace.

"No! To the devil with you!" shouted Sabina, shoving something large toward him.

Hearing this fracas, Millicent wished fervently that she had left the hold a few minutes before. Her mind whirled with terror, and it was all she could do to concentrate on moving slowly and silently. A scream was at the back of her throat. Whoever this Helmut was, he had killed passengers on this ship, and others as well. He would not hesitate to kill Sabina, or her. She saw the outline of the hold door ahead of her, and it seemed that it was miles away.

"You will regret this!" Helmut vowed as Sabina stumbled away through the darkness.

Let me live through this, God, Millicent thought as she

crept toward the door, and I promise I'll try very hard to believe in You, no matter what else happens. She knew she had to get out of the hold, and that meant ignoring what was taking place behind her. Resolutely she shut out the sounds she heard and kept moving, staying out of the patches of light as much as she could. She was less than ten feet from the door when a hand sunk into her shoulder and an arm went around her neck.

"I thought so," muttered Helmut as he dragged Millicent backward.

"Let go—" Millicent shouted, kicking vigorously.

Helmut's arm tightened across Millicent's throat. "Be quiet, Miss Cathcart. Or I will silence you."

His fingers were hard as steel, his arm wiry and strong. Millicent squirmed once and gagged as the pressure on her neck increased.

"I think," said Helmut a trifle breathlessly, "that it had better be this."

Millicent heard a metal door open, and before she could protest she was thrust inside a tall, narrow box, almost the size and shape of a coffin. As she started to shove the door, she heard a lock snap into place.

"Let your magician friend try to explain this," Helmut said from the other side of the door.

Millicent saw a number of round holes in the front of the box that enclosed her, and she realized with sinking horror where she was—Helmut had trapped her in the Iron Maiden.

18

For one eternal instant, Millicent was paralyzed with dread. She could only stare at the holes where the spikes would push through, seven across, seventeen high. "That's one hundred nineteen spikes," she muttered to herself, and the sound of her own voice broke the spell that immobilized her.

Behind her, she could hear the crank squeak, and she knew that Helmut Granz—whoever he was—had started moving the spikes forward.

Think! she ordered herself in her mind. There was not much time before she would be within range of the long, lethal steel spikes. One hundred nineteen of them, she reminded herself, and just as swiftly ordered herself to stop. All of them would not pass through her. She had to suppress a giddy desire to laugh. Think! If there is a way out of here, she thought sternly, it is in good sense and quick action. She tried to recall what Anton had said to

Sabina about the Iron Maiden. It was something about fit. As Millicent forced herself to look at the front of the cabinet, she tried rationally to estimate where her greatest danger lay. All the spikes would not go through her, she reasoned, and most of them would not touch her. At least her hands were not confined as Sabina's had appeared to be when the illusion was performed. It *is* an illusion, Millicent insisted. Sabina wasn't really transfixed by spikes, and if she could get out of it, Millicent would, too.

The mechanism groaned as the spikes moved closer.

Millicent decided that there were five spikes that would place her in actual danger. She could avoid the others by standing on tiptoe and holding her arms out to the side. Therefore, she had to concentrate on those five spikes. She ground her teeth together and turned around to face the advancing back panel.

"It's locked, Miss Cathcart," said Helmut with satisfaction. "Struggle if you like, there is no way out."

"Be damned to you," Millicent yelled, astonished at her own temerity. She had never sworn aloud before—she had also never had anyone try to kill her before, she reminded herself, and made her hands reach out to the spikes.

They were very solid, and showed no inclination to give. They were not hinged, nor did they collapse into themselves. That was two possibilities exhausted. She took a firmer hold of the highest of the five, the one that would penetrate her skull. She had one more hope. She turned the spike hard.

At first nothing happened other than the closer movement of the panel, and then the spike began to unscrew.

It was all Millicent could do to remain silent. She wanted

to shout with relief. Working as quickly as possible, she began to unscrew the spike, holding it in her hand as she loosened and removed the second, and then the third.

She knew she would have to make sounds or at least wriggle and kick in the Iron Maiden, or Helmut might stop and investigate, which would be more dangerous than her present situation. She managed to give a yelp as she unscrewed the fourth spike.

"You should have left well enough alone, Miss Cathcart. You might have saved yourself all this had you not tried to take matters into your own hands."

"Don't hurt me!" Millicent whimpered, sounding very silly to her own ears.

"I'm sorry it was necessary. But you interfered."

Millicent decided she had better do something more, so she kicked and screeched, hoping the unknown murderer would be convinced she was feeling the first touch of the spikes. She had the fifth spike unscrewed and for the first time she wanted to cry. Instead, she let out what she hoped was a blood-curdling scream, then gave way to the sobs she could not hold back.

"It is unfortunate you had to end this way," said Helmut, giving a final couple of turns to the crank in the back of the Iron Maiden.

It was almost impossible for Millicent to keep silent, but she marshaled all her strength, not moving, hardly breathing, only the tears in her eyes refusing to cease. She pressed her face against the metal front of the cabinet, trusting that Helmut would not crank the back panel all the way forward so that the spikes protruded through the holes in the front. There was no reason for him to do this, and Millicent hoped fervently that he would stop. If he inspected the front of the Iron Maiden, he would see that there was no blood, and no spikes showing where her body was. She did not want to imagine what he might try then.

A sound from another part of the hold caught Millicent's attention and distracted Helmut. "A pity you had to be done away with," said Helmut in a very calm manner. "You were a bright child. If only you hadn't been so curious."

Millicent listened to this in disbelief. She wanted to call out, to challenge this cruel, casual man who regarded his crimes so lightly. She remained still, and her mind was filled with the enormity of her danger. Now that she was relatively safe, she felt weak. While she had had something to occupy her mind—how to save herself—it had been possible not to think of how close she had come to dying, but now she could not dismiss or minimize the hideous possibilities. If she had not figured out how the illusion was done, if Helmut had been faster operating the crank, if Helmut had bothered to check the front of the Iron Maiden . . . "Stop it, stop it, stop it," she whispered. She wondered if she was going to faint.

A door closed, and then another opened, and once again Millicent held herself as still as she could, and every second that passed felt intolerably long.

The new arrival made no effort at concealing himself, and even once whistled a bit.

Millicent took a long, shattering breath, and then with all the power left in her lungs, she bellowed, *"Help!"*

The whistling stopped at once.

"Help!" Millicent cried again, feeling suddenly very sleepy

and with the most dreadful stomachache she had ever had.

Steps came nearer, and a voice called out, "Where are you?"

"Anton!" Millicent shouted. "The Iron Maiden!"

Hasty steps approached. "Jibben! Bring a crowbar!"

Millicent let the spikes she had been clutching in her left hand drop with a resounding clatter.

"And turn the lights on. It's dark as a well in here!" He was behind the Iron Maiden, and he reached for the crank, turning it quickly to pull the spikes back so that Millicent would have more room to move in the coffin-sized metal box.

"Anton, let me out of here!" Millicent ordered him, forgetting all she had ever been taught about manners.

"Millicent!" The crank stopped turning. "Millicent?"

"Yes; yes! Just let me *out*!" And to her horror, she began to weep once more, her sobs ragged in the aftermath of her fear.

Jibben came from another part of the hold, saying, "Here's the crowbar. I could go to your cabin for your keys. What do you—"

"Millicent's locked in there," Anton interrupted brusquely. "Get that lock broken."

"It might damage—"

"Get it open!" Anton commanded.

At once there was a sharp impact that set Millicent's teeth on edge, followed by the nerve-wrenching sound of metal groaning against metal.

"Millicent," said Anton, only inches away from her. "Are you all right?"

"Yes. I'm . . . not hurt." She tried to keep from crying but could not.

"What on earth happened?" He made an effort to lower his voice so that she would not be more upset than she was already.

"I don't know," Jibben said as he strove with the crowbar. The lock squealed and moaned under the pressure.

"Get that thing off," Anton urged. "Millicent, hold on. It won't be long."

"I'm trying. Not much more to go," said the imperturbable Jibben, leaning on the crowbar more forcefully.

"Please," whispered Millicent. She felt her knees tremble and temples throb.

With one more shove, the lock burst open. The Iron Maiden lurched at the strain, and for a moment it teetered on three legs while Anton reached to steady it. Jibben pulled the door open and Millicent stumbled out.

"Thank you, thank you," she murmured, one hand coming up to shield her face. "Thank you."

"How on earth . . . ?" Anton asked, putting his arm around her shoulder. "Are you all right?"

"Yes," she said shakily. "No." To her dismay, on top of her tears, she started to hiccup. "Oh, no."

"Here," Anton said, taking her by the arm and leading her away from the Iron Maiden. "Sit down and I'll get you something to drink."

"I don't need that," she said, grateful to sit down. She did not quite believe she had really got out of the Iron Maiden, that she was still alive.

"Jibben, go get some tea for us, will you," Anton said, ignoring her protestations.

Jibben obeyed promptly, saying as he left the hold, "I'm

going to speak to Captain Symington. This has gone far enough."

"It has," Anton agreed grimly as he sat on the bench beside Millicent. "What were you doing here?" he asked, watching her with concern.

Millicent made up her mind to stop crying, and this time her eyes obeyed. Soon all that was left was sniffles and hiccups. She cleared her throat. "I wanted to find something out."

"What?" Anton asked, prodding her with his word.

"It was . . ." Everything was still somewhat confused in her thoughts, so Millicent took another deep breath and tried to present her information more coherently. "I'd been talking to Miss Gordon. She said she thought she had seen someone floating in the dark corner of her cabin . . . in the air . . . and I wanted to find out how it could be done." She had only hiccuped twice telling this, which she hoped was an improvement.

"You thought that I . . . ?" Anton began, aghast.

"No," Millicent said, wishing she could laugh at such an absurd notion. "I thought you or Jibben could tell me how it was done. When I got here, I overheard Sabina talking to someone. That's how it started." Telling the rest took longer than she had reckoned it would, and it was difficult to describe being locked in the Iron Maiden.

"Good for you," Anton approved when she explained how she had figured out the trick with the spikes. "If anything had happened to you, Millicent . . ."

"Well, it didn't" was her gruff reply.

"I've got to find Sabina," Anton said a few seconds later. "She has some questions to answer."

"Yes," Millicent agreed with vehemence.

"I'll make sure Jibben stays with you. I don't want you by yourself until we reach port. This killer has to be stopped. And he cannot be let near you again."

"The name is Helmut Granz," Millicent said, hating the sound of it as she spoke.

"German, by the sound of it, but that might not mean much. Granz . . . Granz. I know it from somewhere." He stood up, calling for Jibben. "I want you to stay with Millicent; Sabina has to explain a few things to me."

Jibben, who had come back from his errand and stood in the doorway, nodded once, saying nothing.

"I want you to remain with her. She could easily have lost her life for me, and that is a debt I cannot repay." He started toward the door, then looked back at Millicent, who was sitting on the bench, hunched over and dishiveled, feeling more tired than she ever had in her life. "I mean that, Millicent."

"You don't have to," she said, trying very hard to keep alert. "I came here on my own."

"You were acting for me," Anton said very seriously. "I will never forget that." He gestured to Jibben and then he was gone.

"You should be with him," Millicent said slowly. "That Granz person thinks I'm dead. He won't bother with me. It's Anton he's after, and Anton doesn't have anyone with him. If there are any more killings, how will he be able to prove he didn't do them?"

"There will not be any more murdered for a little while. The assassin dare not risk it. There would be too many questions asked. Now that Anton is under suspicion, everyone watches him, and that can be very useful, in its way."

Millicent favored Jibben with a wan smile. "I don't want to be alone. I don't agree with you, but . . ."

Jibben shrugged. "Anton has given me my orders; I am bound to obey him."

"All right," Millicent said, letting herself be persuaded. "But we'd better tell the Captain about this. Anton won't, will he?" It was a shrewd guess, but an accurate one.

"No, he would have to reveal too much," Jibben said with very little inflection.

"Well, that's letting pride get ahead of sense if your life's in danger," said Millicent with indisputable understanding. "Besides, I *know* that the killer isn't Anton, and that he *is* Helmut Granz. The Captain needs to know that, doesn't he?"

"It's reasonable," said Jibben, and Millicent was not entirely sure he wasn't teasing her.

"All right, then," she said, making herself get to her feet and straighten her clothing as best she could. Her hair, she knew, was in complete disarray, but she decided she would leave it as it was, and if that shocked the Captain, then so much the better. She walked toward the door, her feet heavy as anvils.

They found Captain Symington some twenty minutes later, seated behind the desk in his private quarters. He greeted Millicent with some constraint.

"What seems to be the matter, Miss Cathcart?" He watched Jibben with some suspicion.

"Is there a passenger on this ship, or a crew member, named Helmut Granz?" Millicent asked without any polite exchanges.

"Why do you want to know that?" Captain Symington countered, with some disapproval.

"Because that's the name of the man who has done the killings." She folded her arms, trusting that she had gained all of Captain Symington's attention.

"What makes you think that?" Captain Symington inquired, his disapproval becoming irritation.

"I heard him say it," she answered. "I heard him admit to the murders." She sensed that she was being humored, and it infuriated her.

"I see. And how did this happen?" Captain Symington began to refill his fountain pen from the inkwell on his desk.

"It happened just before he locked me in the Iron Maiden and tried to kill me because of what I'd overheard." She said this brazenly, determined to convince the Captain.

Ink spattered over the wide blotter and the letter the Captain had been writing. "What?"

This time Millicent knew she had his undivided attention.

19

By the time she had finished telling Captain Symington what had taken place in the hold, the Captain's face was grim. He interrupted her only once, and that was to order a copy of the passenger manifest and a complete listing of the men on the ship. He had heard the rest in appalled silence.

"The man won't be listed," Jibben predicted when the chief steward brought the lists that the Captain had requested.

"Of course he will," Captain Symington said testily.

"If he is, it will not be under that name," Jibben stated, unperturbed. "Men of that kind never do announce themselves."

"Except to their victims?" suggested Captain Symington with a tightening of his mouth.

"It's boasting," said Millicent. "He was boasting to Sabina. He said that he had killed more people than Jack the Ripper."

This time Captain Symington swallowed hard before speaking. "He will have to be found, whoever he is."

"And soon," said Jibben.

"But why the magician?" the Captain wondered aloud. "Why him?"

Millicent hesitated, looking once at Jibben, and then said, "It's not because of what he is, but what he was." She took a deep breath. "He doesn't like people to know about him, but since that's why all this is happening, perhaps you should know."

"If it has anything to do with what takes place on my ship, I most certainly should know," said Captain Symington, glaring. "And I warn you, if it is a matter of crime—"

"Not that he committed," Jibben interrupted.

"You'd best explain that," Captain Symington told them both.

"There were attempts made on Anton's life three years ago in London, I think for the same reason as he is being discredited now," said Jibben.

"And why is that?" said Captain Symington impatiently. "I know that you are very loyal to him, and you realize this makes what you tell me suspicious." He paused as Jibben watched him. "I also know that Gypsies are not noted for truthfulness."

"Next you'll tell me that I'm part of the treachery," said Jibben with anger.

"That's ridiculous!" Millicent broke in.

"No, the Captain does right to reserve his judgment," Jibben said, astounding the Captain. "I will tell you this, sir, and you can make up your mind from it. Anton found me stealing from his stage properties just after he came to England, almost seven years ago. He took me in, had me educated, and trained and fed me. You may not have a very high opinion of Gypsies, but you can assume I have no reason to wish harm on the Duke."

Captain Symington blinked. "Is that a nickname?"

"No," said Jibben bluntly, "it is a title."

"Am I to infer that Anton has some bar sinister claim?" asked the Captain carefully.

"He's not illegitimate," said Millicent, who understood the reference. "He's abdicated, but he was an Archduke."

The Captain gave a little disbelieving laugh. "Oh, really?"

"Yes," said Jibben.

"It's true," said Millicent. "And that's why the killer is aboard. If he doesn't succeed in framing Anton for the murders, he'll probably try to kill him." Her throat felt very tight. "He was willing to kill me simply because of what I overheard, even though most courts would not allow me to testify."

"I see," said the Captain. "Well, you'll understand if I prefer to speak to Anton about this?" He stood. "Miss Cathcart, I am in no way minimizing your danger, the terrible risk you took, or your intrepidity. I am also not questioning your sincerity, but I will have to look into all of this more closely. If you'll be good enough to excuse me? I'll have Chief Steward Roman escort you to your cabin. I'm sure you must want to rest. Jibben, if you will come with me, I'll have a word or two with your employer."

"Fine. He's likely to be put out for us telling you, but I can listen to that." Jibben looked at Millicent. "You better get her a bite to eat before sending her off to bed, Captain. She looks burned to the socket."

"You're right." He rang a bell on his desk, and when Chief Steward Roman answered the summons, he said, "Take Miss Cathcart to the Grand Salon and see that she has something to eat, and then escort her to her cabin with my compliments to her aunt." With that, he left his quarters, Jibben following after him.

Chief Steward Roman gave a hard stare to Millicent, then said, "If you will come with me, I will see to you."

"Thank you," Millicent said, her attitude turning sullen. She was exhausted, her head still ached, her mind was in turmoil, and someone named Helmut Granz had tried to kill her. It took all of her self-possession for her to rise and go with Chief Steward Roman.

The Grand Salon was almost deserted, for at this time of day few passengers might be found there under ordinary conditions. Now most of the first-class passengers spent much of their time in the cabins, hoping to avoid more tragedy. So it was that only an elderly Frenchman, Mister and Missus Emmory, and Milton Homes were there to see Chief Steward Roman bring Millicent in for a late lunch.

"Goodness!" exclaimed Missus Emmory as she caught sight of Millicent. "Whatever happened to you, child?"

Milton Homes jumped visibly.

"Your aunt was looking for you a short time ago," said Mister Emmory. "She and Missus Dovecote went off to your cabin together."

Where they are probably consulting Big Wolf or Ling Lu about me, thought Millicent huffily. "I'll join her directly," said Millicent, trying to mind her manners. "Right now I need some soup."

"We'll see you have a little more than that," Chief Steward Roman cajoled her. "The Captain expects me to take care of you."

For Millicent, such words still had a sinister feeling, and she cleared her throat. "Thank you. I am a little distressed." As she sat down, she reminded herself sternly that she could say nothing of her ordeal, for that might compromise the investigation and she would be as exposed as she had ever been.

As Chief Steward Roman started toward the kitchens, Mister Homes got up, much agitated, and said, "I have to speak to you. It's urgent."

"All right," answered the Chief Steward, and indicated the alcove near the kitchen. The two men stepped into it, where they conversed in undertones.

Millicent watched the two, seeing Mister Homes emphasize some troublesome point with a sudden, downward chop of his hand, while Chief Steward Roman shook his head emphatically. Millicent wished they would finish whatever they had to say so that she could have something to eat before she fell asleep where she sat.

Whatever the resolution of the discussion—if there was one—Chief Steward Roman did not spend much time with Mister Homes. He was soon going to the kitchens and came back in less than five minutes with a bowl of Swedish cherry soup. "Here," he said to Millicent, not as cordially as before. "There will be more in a few minutes."

Millicent thanked him and started to eat. Ordinarily she liked cherry soup, but now it seemed much too sweet, and she took no more than half a dozen spoonfuls before she wanted no more.

By that time, Chief Steward Roman had brought her some very thin-sliced ham and chicken on a bed of spinach leaves with a few pickled beets as a garnish. "Do you want any more of the soup?" he asked in a surly way.

"I don't think so, no. It was good of you to bring it to me. I'm sorry my appetite is a disappointment. Please tell the chef it is my fatigue, not his cooking." She hardly listened to herself, and the words came out automatically. Her headache was worse.

When she had eaten half of the meat, she set that plate aside as well and got up.

"You don't look well, child," sympathized Missus Emmory. "And your dress is . . . disordered."

"I had an accident," said Millicent. "I need to lie down for a little while, that's all."

"I see," said Missus Emmory.

"I doubt it," Millicent responded, astonished at herself. "I didn't mean—"

"Miss Cathcart is upset," said Mister Emmory in a placating way. "We can talk to her later, dear. She'll be restored after a rest." He smiled at Millicent in a manner that was intended to reassure and only made Millicent itch to throw something at him. The ferocity of her reaction was startling to her more than to the others, and she began a complicated apology. "I'm sorry. I don't know what's come over me, only that I'm very tired and it's made me lose track of—"

"That's all right," said Missus Emmory. "You run along to your cabin and have a rest."

"Yes; I will," said Millicent, deciding not to wait for the chief steward to take her. It was not far to her cabin, and she knew that at this time of day, with so many people about, Helmut Granz would not dare make a second attempt on her.

"Give our regards to your aunt," said Mister Emmory. "And don't you worry about anything. We know what happens to girls when they are overtired."

Millicent was too tired to take issue with this. She left the Grand Salon and went straight to her cabin, hardly pausing to knock before she let herself in.

Mehitabel looked up from a deep conversation with Missus Dovecote. "Goodness gracious, Millicent," she scolded, "where on earth have you been? We've been waiting for you for the last hour and a half. I've been distracted with worry. Auralia and I were about to consult the spirits."

Missus Dovecote, resplendent in an afternoon ensemble of mauve with a trim of ecru lace, gave Millicent a reproachful look. "Your aunt has been beside herself. You should not have been so inconsiderate."

"I . . . I lost track of the time," said Millicent lamely, suddenly unwilling to talk about what had taken place in the hold. "I'm sorry if I worried you."

"And look at your dress. What have you been doing?" Mehitabel rose from the sofa. "Your hair is in disarray as well. Tell me this instant what—"

"It's nothing for you to worry about," said Millicent. "You can ask Big Wolf if you don't believe me."

"How do you know about Big Wolf?" demanded Missus Dovecote, quite scandalized.

"I watched you in your trance," Millicent confessed, too worn out to do anything else. Yesterday spying on their séances had seemed like good entertainment; today it was nothing more than a silly and childish prank.

"That was very naughty," said Missus Dovecote, prepared to go on at length.

Mehitabel held up her hand, stopping her friend's tirade. "I can see that Millicent needs time to herself," she said with unexpected compassion. "When do you want to be wakened, Millicent?"

"In time for supper, I suppose," said Millicent, opening the door to the bedroom. "Go on talking: you won't disturb me."

"As you like. If you want to talk with me later, I am eager to hear what you have to say," she told her niece. "Sleep well, dear."

"Thanks," murmured Millicent as she shut the door. She did not bother to undress, but lay down on her bed and closed her eyes. She was asleep almost at once.

In her dreams she was pursued and confined in strange and terrifying places by ogres and wizards who menaced her in frightening ways. She awoke with a start three hours later, and was not able to recall at first just where she was or why she was fully clothed.

Mehitabel came in at once, turning on the light as she did. "Is there anything wrong, Millicent?"

"No," she answered as all her memories rushed back at her.

"Captain Symington was here a little while ago. He and I had a talk. I can understand why you appeared as you did. You did a very brave thing."

"I didn't feel very brave," said Millicent, abashed.

"No, one never does. That's what makes it so daunting." She came across the room and sat on the edge of the other bed. "The Captain has requested that you come to his quarters before you go in to dinner. He has a few questions—"

"Oh, no," Millicent interrupted. She wanted very much to put the whole experience behind her.

"I gather that there has been no success in locating the assistant, Sabina. He says that they must fear the worst, because of all that has gone before." She seemed very calm, but her eyes kept moving restlessly. "I gave him my word that you would visit him."

"If I must," Millicent growled, then remembered herself. "I guess I'd better get dressed. Will you help me do something with my hair? I don't want to touch it."

"Yes, in a moment," said Mehitabel. "I have something more to say. While I was listening to Captain Symington, I was very angry at first for what you had done, and I wanted to correct your behavior. Then, when I had thought about it for a while, I realized that what troubled me the most was that I would never have been in a predicament like yours, and that was what was most vexing." She looked down at her hands in her lap. "You see, I should never have courage enough to do what you have done."

Millicent felt her face go bright red. "Aunt Mehitabel . . ."

"I know this about myself. It does not please me, but I cannot deny it." She straightened her back. "That is what I wanted to say. Now I'll help you get ready for dinner. The Captain will be very glad to see you." She got up and went to get pins and brushes.

Half an hour later, Millicent, dressed in a neat velvet frock with her hair drawn back from her face and caught up in a cascade of curls high on the back of her head, went to the Captain's quarters. She was far more apprehensive about seeing him now than she had been that afternoon.

Captain Symington himself admitted her, and she found Anton seated near the big desk. He rose as she came in; Millicent was flustered and delighted at this courtesy.

"You're looking more yourself," said the Captain tactfully.

"Thank you, I've rested and my aunt helped me get ready." She turned to smile at Anton. "What happened while I was asleep?"

"Very little," he said with a discouraged sigh as he held one of the other chairs for her. "Jibben is still searching for Sabina. We're all afraid that Helmut Granz might have found her ahead of us."

"And that she's dead?" Millicent asked, determined not to flinch at her own question.

"It's possible," said Captain Symington. "I've been speaking with . . . Anton for some time about how best to flush out this killer. I don't want to expose Miss Sabina to any more violence; I don't want to be responsible for any more deaths on my ship." His face was harsh with resolution.

"Luckily, you've taken the Captain's suspicions off me," said Anton. "Helmut Granz—I've remembered the man and the name, thank goodness—is not as unknown as he fancies he is; Captain Symington has been warned about him by European police before, and in London, when I was shot, there was speculation that Granz might have been behind the attempt." He nodded toward the Captain. "But, sadly, we don't know very much about him. He's very . . . shadowy."

"From what I heard," said Millicent, casting her mind back to that overheard conversation—was it only that afternoon?—"he wanted to take something of Anton's, something more than a spangle off Sabina's costume. Apparently Sabina had said she would loan him some of the magical equipment."

"Her suitor?" Anton said. "There was a tall man courting her, and that might . . ." He glanced up at the Captain for a reaction. "Someone in second class, I think."

"I'll speak to my chief steward," said Captain Symington.

Millicent studied her hands and realized that she had bitten all of her fingernails off to the quick in the last hour. "Captain, I don't think it means anything, but when your chief steward escorted me to the Grand Salon, he got into a private discussion with Mister Homes. I don't know what it was about, but you may want to talk to him. Mister Homes was probably just scared. He's such a nervous, quiet man." She looked toward Anton. "He's frightened of his own shadow, I think."

"Strange fellow," Anton agreed, not paying much attention.

Captain Symington had half risen when there was a knock on the door, and almost immediately it was opened by Jibben, who was actually smiling.

"Your pardon," he said to the three, "but I thought you'd want to know: I've found Sabina."

20

"Is she . . ." Anton asked, not speaking his fears.

"Quite alive. She was hiding out in the laundry. It seems one of the workers there is also from Whitechapel and they have a connection of some nature." Jibben grinned. "I was sure she'd go to ground. Knowing her, it was likely she'd find some help."

"I'll speak to the crewman," said Captain Symington.

"No reason to do that, sir," said Jibben. "He didn't know he was doing anything wrong. He was told that Anton was mad at her for not helping him out. He looked at Anton. "You know what she can be like."

"I certainly do," Anton said as he got to his feet. "Where is she now? I want to find out more about this beau of hers."

"I have her in my cabin. No one saw her and she's promised to keep still. I locked her in, as an extra precaution. We'd better be quick, though. No saying but what that suitor of hers will try to locate her."

Captain Symington put his hand on his bell, then thought better of it. "The fewer who know of this, the better. We'd best tend to this at once."

"Very good," Anton approved as he held the chair for Millicent. "Do you want to stay with your aunt while we do this?"

"No. I want to follow it to the end." She was stubborn enough that no one disputed her right to accompany them.

Sabina was nearly distraught by the time Jibben returned to his cabin with Captain Symington, Anton, and Millicent. She turned on him at once, upbraiding him for leaving her alone. "What would have happened if Helmut had found me? Have you thought about that?"

"He couldn't pass through a locked door," Anton said, affecting a boredom that his restless movements denied.

"He doesn't have to, does he? He's got a pass key from someone on the crew." She nodded at the startled reaction her revelation brought. "Ah, so you, mister high-and-mighty Duke, didn't know that? Well, some of us aren't lucky enough to be related to half the noble houses of Europe. We have to find other ways to get on in the world." She tossed her head, her defiance covering near panic.

"A pass key?" said Captain Symington quietly. "Where did he get it? There are only two, or there are supposed to be only two."

"He didn't bother to tell me. He wanted a few things out of Anton's show. They weren't being used, and he was sweet as new honey when he wanted something from me." She stopped suddenly and began to weep. "He lied to me. Made me think that he didn't care about where I came from or what I've done. He was a real gentleman at first. It was only later—"

"Yes, yes," Captain Symington said, not able to sympathize with her. "It's very unfortunate. But we need to know as much as possible about this beau of yours, and the sooner the better."

Millicent felt sorry for Sabina, who was far more frightened than she was willing to admit. She said, "If you can tell us these things, then we can stop him before he kills anyone else. If you help, it could be very good for you. The police would give you recognition for your bravery, and certainly everyone on board would be grateful to you." She had heard her mother handle a difficult servant in this way, but she was still amazed when it worked.

"Would they?" Sabina asked, her vanity stronger than her fear.

"Most certainly," said Anton, with a slight nod to the Captain.

"I, for one," said Captain Symington, taking up his cue, "would thank you publicly."

"Oh," said Sabina, considering the possibilities. "Would it mean being in danger any longer?"

"Nothing more than staging another small performance," said Anton, who greeted the startled looks of the others in the cabin with a knowing wink. "I think it's time we used some of this Helmut's magic on him for a change."

"I don't know as this is a good idea," said Captain Symington. "Most of the passengers are skittish now, and they are not very tolerant of your performing."

"Good," said Anton unexpectedly. "Then we can turn their feelings to our advantage in unmasking this Granz. And, Sabina," he pressed on, "you would not have to expose yourself for an instant. You would be safe the entire time."

"What did you have in mind?" asked Jibben. "Can we do it on a rolling ship?"

"I think so. I was thinking of a small version of our 'Pepper's Ghost.' " He smiled at the Captain. "Let us plan this for tomorrow afternoon. We can be ready by then. The performance will be brief, but with any luck, we'll have the man. If we don't, nothing will be lost but a little time."

"We might spend the time investigating instead," suggested Captain Symington.

"I would hope you'd do both," said Anton. Then he glanced at Millicent. "Do you think you can persuade your aunt and Missus Dovecote to attend another magic performance?"

"I believe so. What is 'Pepper's Ghost' about?" she asked.

"Just what it says: spirits appear and disappear. It's very impressive. Pepper used it in stage plays; I believe the illusion has been used in *Hamlet* for the ghost."

Captain Symington shook his head. "Very well, I can see you're determined. I'm afraid that once you start to perform there is little protection I or my men can offer you."

"That's all right. I'm the only one exposed." He held his hand out to Sabina. "Cry truce, won't you? It would benefit us both if you will cooperate with us."

She tossed her head and did her best to recapture her

saucy manner. "Very well, then, but see that I'm thanked proper for what I do."

"You will have my thanks," said Captain Symington dryly.

"Publicly," she insisted.

"Naturally," the Captain capitulated as gracefully as he could.

"Then I'll do it. You see that he does, Duke," she added to Anton.

"I'll be pleased to," said Anton. "In the meantime, we must try to find a way to set up the illusion. Jibben, let's go back to the Grand Ballroom and see what we can do there."

Jibben nodded. "I'll tend to it at once."

"And I think," Anton added, "that you' best remain here, Sabina. We don't want word of finding you to get around. It might be useful to order the search continued, so that Granz will not be alerted. If he is as good at his work as he's supposed to be, he'll be especially sensitive to rumors." As they reached the door, Anton paused. "Something must be done about the lock."

"I'll see it's tended to. I can always order a stricter watch be kept on your assistant," Captain Symington said. In another voice, he went on, "A pass key. Who would have thought of that?"

"In stage magic, Captain, remember that the simplest and most obvious solution is the correct one. The rest is showmanship and misdirection. I'd venture a guess that Granz is very good at both in his way." He motioned to Millicent to join them. "I'm relying on you to convince the passengers to attend the performance. You're young enough that the worst they'll suspect of you is that you're biased on my behalf, which, thank goodness, you are."

Millicent felt a trifle disappointed that this was all that Anton wished of her, and at the same time she was glad that she would not have to take any more risks like the one she had taken in the Iron Maiden. "I'll do what I can to convince Missus Dovecote, and I'll speak to Miss Gordon. That's a start." She wanted both the Captain and Anton to be aware of her determination, and so she added as they left Jibben's cabin, "If you like, I can make an announcement after dinner."

"I'll do that," said Captain Symington firmly. "It's part of my responsibilities."

"All right," Millicent said, still trying to think of other things she could do.

Aunt Mehitabel was waiting in the Grand Salon for Millicent, and when her niece arrived, she all but pounced on her. "What did the Captain want? It has to do with those horrid murders, I'm sure of it." Her outburst attracted the attention of several of the other passengers in the Grand Salon, and they all fell silent while Millicent answered.

"No, there was a question about the Incredible Anton doing one more performance." This information was greeted with mutters and other signs of disapproval. "It seems," she went on more forcefully, "that there is some special magical trick that Anton might do which the Captain especially wishes to see because it might shed some light on how the murders were done."

The reaction this time was better than Millicent had hoped.

"The fellow has nerve, no doubt about it," said one of the British passengers with reluctant respect. "Those stage boys, they're up to anything."

"What can it be this time?" wondered one of the German passengers.

"What an absurd thing!" Mehitabel said. "He might as well put the noose around his neck with his own hands. Although he can probably escape from that, too."

"You all still assume he is the killer," said Millicent in her unruffled way. "I'm looking forward to seeing this trick."

Miss Gordon, who had a small glass of sherry in one hand, shuddered. "Trick! You can't appreciate how awful such an experience can be. No one can until they experience it."

Millicent thought of the Iron Maiden and the long steel spikes. "You're probably right," she said sweetly.

"How terrible that we should all be at the mercy of such a killer!" cried out one of the elderly Frenchwomen. "It is one thing to have such persons killing the heads of Balkan states and trying to shoot the Tsar, but when they start choosing victims at random, then that is another matter entirely."

Millicent listened to this, and said, "All the more reason to be diverted by Anton's performance. Most of you think he might be guilty and I know that he is innocent."

"You're a mere child," said a portly Swede. "You are not able to understand these things."

"Well, whether or not he is guilty, we might as well enjoy the entertainment. It's bad enough to brood on these crimes without any alleviation, but to deny ourselves amusements, well!" She wanted to shout at them all, to tell them everything she had learned, and castigate them for their prejudice and blindness, but she did not dare, for that might alert Granz, and then they would all be at the killer's mercy once more.

Mehitabel echoed Millicent's tone at once. "Very true. I recall when Mister Reynes passed on, I could think of nothing but my grief and my predicament until I went to a minstrel show, and then the worst of my misery was over." She smiled at her niece. "You're undoubtedly right; we should all avail ourselves of the entertainment. We've had little enough of it the last few days."

This time the general reaction was not so negative as it had been before, and a few of the passengers showed signs of agreeing with Mehitabel.

"The man has gall," said Milton Homes, muttering to no one in particular. "I won't attend, I will say that."

Miss Gordon finished her sherry. "I think I will. Missus Reyns is probably right: we're all in need of a little diversion, and if the Captain believes that it's safe to permit the man to perform, it would be ridiculous to avoid the offering."

Eventually Miss Gordon's good sense was contagious, and by the time everyone retired for the night, some of the earlier jauntiness had returned.

"Can you imagine?" Missus Dovecote said to Mehitabel as they strolled toward their cabins. "That terrible man is being allowed to try his tricks on us again. What can Captain Symington be thinking of? Probably Anton has brought him under his spell."

Millicent was very nearly out of patience with this friend of her aunt's. "I think we're in far less danger from Anton than we are from those aboard who create rumors and spread them," she said pointedly.

"How true!" exclaimed Missus Dovecote, missing Millicent's intent completely. "I've always said that rumormakers and rumormongers are the worst of a bad breed. Your niece is a most astute young lady, Mehitabel."

"Yes, she is," said Mehitabel. "I hope you sleep well, Auralia, and that Mister Dovecote passes a good night."

"Thank you," said Missus Dovecote effusively. "You're very kind." She kissed the air near Mehitabel's cheek, and then fluttered along the hallway to her cabin door.

"I have to get up early," said Millicent once she and her aunt were alone.

"If that's necessary, then by all means," said Mehitabel. "I only hope you won't come to any harm while you help your friend."

"So do I," said Millicent with feeling. She undressed quickly and washed with habitual thoroughness while Mehitabel took time to give her hair the five hundred strokes with a brush that was expected of her and any well-groomed woman of her age.

"Do you think that you will find out who the murderer is?" asked Mehitabel as Millicent got into her nightgown.

"I hope so," she answered cautiously. "I think there's a very good chance. So do Anton and Captain Symington."

"That must be a great relief to you," said Mehitabel as she went to the cramped bathroom they shared.

"I'm very tired, Aunt Mehitabel. I just want to sleep." Millicent got into bed and pulled the covers up around her head. She was determined to get some sleep, and thought that, as tired as she was, she would slip into her dreams as soon as her head touched the pillow.

But by midnight—she heard the ship's bells chime the

eight strokes that marked the end of the watch—she was still awake, her thoughts alive with recollections of the experiences of the day. As soon as she closed her eyes, she felt the walls of the Iron Maiden close around her again, and she feared to listen in case the ominous whine of the crank should reach her. Almost at once, she would wake up again, her eyes wide in denial, her pulse racing, making her head ache.

Once she thought she saw a shape in the corner of the room, and heard a voice, insinuating and low, speak her name. If only she recognized that voice! Then she would have a name to put with the unseen figure of Helmut Granz.

She got up and washed her face, then had another glass of water. She told herself as sensibly as she could that there was no reason for her to be afraid anymore, that by this time tomorrow the identity of the killer would be known and she would have no reason to be afraid, but it did little good. She lay awake, staring at the ceiling, her eyes aching with exhaustion and her mind burning with memories. She thought about Anton, and his memory of the death of his brothers and father and uncle, and wondered how many nights he had gone without sleep when he was a child.

By morning she had drifted into a fitful and uneasy slumber that left her more tired than she had been before. Her body felt strange to her, as if it belonged to someone else and she was only borrowing it for a time. She tried to laugh about this, but her humor had deserted her, and she only longed for the end of her ordeal to come at last. She made herself rise and dress, her attention focused on the performance that was to come in the afternoon.

21

Anton's stage had been draped at the front, masking the lumber that lifted the stage floor almost four feet above the floor of the ballroom. Extra curtains had been hung, deepening the wings, and the main curtain, closed in readiness for the performance, had been swagged in heavy gold cords with tassels.

With the performance scheduled to begin in less than fifteen minutes, half the seats were occupied and many of the passengers could be seen coming in from the Grand Salon. Several of the women had already removed their elaborate afternoon hats in a gesture of courtesy to those who would be sitting behind them.

To Mehitabel's surprise, Millicent did not want to sit in the front row, but indicated that she wished to be in the last.

"I'd think you'd want to watch closely," said Mehitabel, clearly wanting to do so herself.

"It's not the performance I'm intending to watch," Millicent said. "I'm looking for the killer."

Mehitabel shuddered. "I wish you wouldn't remind me of that. It isn't very good conduct to make others uncomfortable." She lifted her hand to wave to Missus Dovecote. "Auralia is very near the front, isn't she?"

"Sit with her, if you'd rather," said Millicent.

"Nonsense; it's my responsibility to remain with you." She signaled to Missus Dovecote, gesturing her toward them. "Join us, why don't you?"

Missus Dovecote did not need more of an invitation. "I'll be delighted," she said as she came up. "But why sit so far back?"

"The Captain asked me to," said Millicent.

"Goodness!" said Missus Dovecote, impressed by this.

"Sit with us, Auralia."

The three chose seats and made themselves as comfortable as they could as the rest of the passengers came into the ballroom. Finally, just before three, the room darkened, and a single light illuminated the front of the stage. In the darkness, a hush fell over the audience, and there was tentative applause as the curtains parted, revealing Anton in full evening dress quite alone on the stage.

"Good afternoon," he said, bowing. "I thank you for the opportunity to show you one more marvel before we reach land, a marvel so extraordinary that you will not believe what you see." He gestured, and there was a puff of smoke in response.

And then, floating behind him, trailing draperies, was the insubstantial figure of Sabina. She appeared to drift through the air, no more aware of her surroundings than the falling leaves of a tree.

A rush of sighs and whispered words went through the audience as Sabina drifted across the stage.

"The man is a wizard, I tell you," Auralia Dovecote whispered to Mehitabel.

"Amazing, isn't it?" said Anton, gesturing toward the apparition that wafted behind him. "How many of you think that we cannot summon the dead back from their distant realm?"

"Big Wolf and Ling Lu! What he could do with them!" Missus Dovecote murmured.

"You see how she goes through obstacles?" He held up a board, hit it sharply to show that it was solid, then lifted it squarely into the path of the drifting shape of Sabina. The draped figure appeared to pass through the board, unhampered by it.

"Those of you who have spent the last few days wondering how locked doors might be breached will find this especially interesting, I daresay."

Millicent, now that she had permitted herself the enjoyment of watching the illusion, began to study the audience.

"They say that those who return from the dead can reveal secrets that are not known to the living." He held up his hand and there was another puff of smoke. "I conjure you!" he addressed the wraith.

This order was greeted by a low moan.

Several members of the audience were showing real agitation at this manifestation. One of the Frenchwomen was fanning herself as if the room had suddenly grown very hot; Missus Emmory had her head pressed against her husband's shoulder; Miss Gordon was leaning forward, her attention very much on the stage.

"I conjure you to reveal the manner of your death and the one who killed you!" Anton's voice was resounding, and the vision gave a long wail, and then spoke while suspended in the air.

"It was my beau!" Sabina's hollow tones announced. "He who called himself Helmut and wooed me with false words. He is the one who brought me to this pass!"

The rustle and mutter in the audience grew louder.

"Why did he do this?" Anton commanded.

"He sought to conceal his guilt in other crimes," Sabina declaimed. "I knew too much, and so he—"

There was a loud report of pistol fire and the crash of shattering glass.

Millicent climbed onto her chair and pointed toward someone in one of the back rows of the audience. "There he is!" she yelled to the Captain's men standing around the ballroom.

Confusion erupted in the audience, and from the stage Anton called out, "Please, ladies and gentlemen, remain in your seats." He repeated this several times as the ship's men closed in on a single figure.

"The doors are locked," shouted the Captain. "You cannot escape, Mister Granz."

A lean man stood up, reaching out for Missus Emmory and brandishing a pistol. "Everyone stop, or I will shoot," warned Milton Homes. Now that he was not hunched over, Millicent saw that he was very nearly as tall as Anton.

A pale head emerged from behind the low draperies at the front of the stage. "It's him!" Sabina accused.

There were more shouts and screams, and many of the passengers tried to get away from where Mister Homes—or Helmut Granz—was struggling with Hope Emmory while her husband tried to wrest her away from the assassin.

Millicent reached down and snatched Mehitabel's purse from her. She hefted it once, testing its weight, and then flung it with all her outrage and determination at the back of Granz's head while Mehitabel shrieked in protest.

The purse struck him a glancing blow, hardly enough to do more than annoy, but it was enough for him to lose his grip on Missus Emmory. Her husband pulled her away and dragged her with him through the tangle of passengers and chairs.

"Stop him!" yelled Millicent.

There was a ferocious babble of voices, and it seemed fleetingly that the chaos would provide an escape for Helmut Granz. Then the ship's men closed in, throwing themselves on the man with a purpose, letting nothing more than a scuffle take place before he was knocked unconscious and his wrists handcuffed.

"Escort Herr Granz to the detention cabin and keep an armed guard on him around the clock. He can pass the rest of the voyage with his accomplice, the former chief steward." Captain Symington then strode to the front of the ballroom and addressed Anton. "Are you all right? And your assistant?"

"A minor cut from flying glass," said Anton, touching his cheek. "My assistant was never in any danger; for once, you saw a trick that truly is done with mirrors. See?" He indicated where she was standing.

"You were very brave to cooperate with us," said Captain Symington, reaching out to take Sabina's hand. "I thank you for all you've done to aid us in the identification and capture of these dangerous men."

Sabina all but simpered, beaming at Captain Symington as she nodded toward the audience. "I was only doing my duty, Captain, and it was a right pleasure to do it for a fine man like you."

One or two of the passengers, realizing that they were no longer in danger, applauded.

Anton shook Captain Symington's hand. "I thank you very much for all you've done, and I apologize for bringing so much misfortune aboard. Had I even suspected, you must believe that—"

"No apology is necessary, Archduke." Captain Symington used Anton's old title very deliberately. "But in the future, I hope that you can convince your political enemies to leave you alone."

The audience was beginning to restore some order among its members, though there was some consternation as Mister Homes was led away by the first officer.

"Who would have thought!" Mehitabel said, staring at the captured assassin. "Such a meek, mild man."

"I knew it had to be one of that sort," Missus Dovecote declared. "How else could he have succeeded so long? The quiet ones are the worst."

Millicent was about to object and remind Missus Dovecote that she had been the most eager to condemn Anton of any aboard when she felt her aunt pinch her elbow. "I have to go get your purse," she said, trying very hard not to give way to her temper.

Mehitabel said, "Thank you, dear. I'll need it."

As Millicent threaded her way among the chairs, she suddenly felt very tired, as if she wanted nothing more than to go to sleep for all of a day and a night. Also, in some way she did not entirely understand, she felt disappointed, and a bit saddened that her adventure was over. She had risked and saved her own life, caught a criminal—school would be dull in comparison. She found the purse on the floor and noticed that some of the beads that decorated it had torn loose. Her aunt would not like that.

"Excuse me," said a voice at her shoulder, and she turned to see Captain Symington. "I hope that you and your aunt will do me the honor of dining with me at my table this evening. I'll have my assistant chief steward deliver a proper invitation, of course."

Millicent blinked. "Thank you," she said automatically, and for once she looked forward to dining with the Captain.

Mehitabel was flattered to hear of the Captain's request, and she said, "Did Haywood arrange this as well?"

"No," Millicent said crisply. "At least, he never has before."

Missus Dovecote smiled warmly. "How fortunate for you, Mehitabel. You must be thrilled by such distinction."

"It is very kind of the Captain," said Mehitabel in her most proper tone, and then she looked back toward the stage. "Hush. Anton has something more to say."

Although the stage was shiny with broken glass, and Anton's footsteps crunched with every pace, he did not appear to be distressed. "Ladies and gentlemen, I thank you for your patience and kindness for bearing with this experiment. My assistant, as you see, is quite well, and she has been very brave to assist in this performance, since we knew from the start that there was more than the usual hazard accompanying this entertainment. As you can undoubtedly tell by now, this illusion is done with mirrors, and for that reason we must ask you to take extra care, since there are bits of glass likely to be underfoot. We trust you will excuse us if we do not proceed to our usual finish." He bowed, and signaled to the Captain.

"Please leave in an orderly fashion," Captain Symington said crisply. "Dinner is at the usual hour, and we have asked the chef to prepare a special dessert in . . . celebration of the apprehension of Helmut Granz, who is, as a few of you know, a very dangerous criminal."

The buzz and murmur of conversation grew louder, and the chairs once again shuffled as the audience rose and began to file toward the door.

Behind them on the stage, Jibben was starting to sweep up the glass, and Sabina was starting to wipe the white makeup from her face.

Anton was seated across the table from Millicent, as they had been on the first evening of the voyage.

"From what my former chief steward has said," the Captain was saying,"the reason that Cuernos was killed was that he had some knowledge of Granz's activities. Several countries have been looking for him over the last four years, and even though he had disguised himself, Granz was afraid that General Cuernos might become suspicious of him because of the killings. Wingham had the misfortune to try to become friendly with Granz, and that was far too risky in so limited an environment as an ocean liner. Vaclav Roman knew of the whole plot and agreed to help Granz, since his political allies had hired Granz to do away with Anton. He even killed the steward and understeward for no greater crime than being Bohemian. Apparently they viewed his return to Europe as a political rather than a professional decision." He looked toward Anton, who had been unusually silent.

"I've been afraid that something like this might happen, ever since I was shot in London," he said quietly. "How I wish the past would remain the past."

Millicent sensed his deep sadness. "Don't let it stop you," she said, hoping that she had found the right words.

Apparently she had, for Anton gave a crooked smile in return. "How did you know? Yes, I admit that I've been toying with the notion of retiring, but I'm afraid that it might be assumed that I was doing that for political reasons as well." He sighed. "I've signed a formal abdication, I've made no attempt to assert any claim in any way, and I have stated many times that I have no ambitions to do so. What more must I do?"

"You could return to America," suggested Millicent. "It's a large enough country that you could stay there and perform for years and years." She cocked her head to the side. "Will you think about it?"

This time Anton's smile was more genuine. "You're determined to save me, aren't you?"

To her own astonishment, Millicent blushed deeply. "I just . . . don't want to see a friend suffer," she said in confusion.

"And to prevent that, you were willing to suffer yourself," said Anton seriously. "By all rights, since I am beholden to you, I ought to take your advice. Perhaps I will. You may be right about this. Heaven knows you've been right about everything else."

"Gracious, your flattery will go to her head," warned Mehitabel playfully.

"Not flattery, Missus Reyns," corrected Anton gently.

"What I offer is the simplest and most honest compliment." There was a movement at his shoulder as one of the waiters brought up a champagne bucket with two iced bottles and four glasses.

As the waiter put one of the glasses at Millicent's place—to Millicent's secret delight—Mehitabel protested.

"Captain, my niece is only fourteen. Surely . . ."

Captain Symington signaled the waiter to open the first bottle. "My dear Missus Reyns, anyone who is adult enough to risk his—or her—life for a friend and to aid in the capture of a dangerous murderer is adult enough for a glass of champagne," he said as the cork popped.

"Allow me," said Anton, rising and taking the bottle from the waiter in order to pour the sparkling wine himself. He remained standing when he had done, and said, lifting his glass, "To friendship."

As the others echoed the toast, he touched the rim of Millicent's glass with his own.